Blurring shapes and s

were always more feelings then images. ...

on her bed, tossing and turning as darkness and fear entered her thoughts. A face swam in front of her, making her heart pound with terror. It was him, the inflictor of pain. Two more faces joined him, the step brothers. Finally, floating above them all was her step father. A silent scream echoed throughout her mind, her fear so intense she had stopped breathing, arched off her bed, her dream catcher spinning wildly. The crystals glittered and shone, the first rays of dawn glinting across her face, allowing peace and calm to flow into her. In her dark dream the moon flooded her vision, before being eclipsed by a giant beast, a creature that would strike terror into grown men but all she felt was pure, unrestranable joy. The enormous wolf loped down to stand beside her, nuzzling her hand gently, licking her with love then with a deafening howl he dived onto the inflictor of pain and the step brothers and the step father, tearing them limb from limb. She was covered in a spray of blood, she could taste it on her lips, feel in dripping from her hair. But she only smiled, her protector, the wolf, was avenging the tremendous hurt the men had inflicted upon her, and destroying the fear that held her frozen in time. When there was nothing left the wolf came back to her, rubbing against her. As the moonlight faded the wolf became a towering man, full of love and devotion withheld just for her, only her, always her. They embraced. The dream shattered with a bellow of anger.

Stinging slaps across her thighs, too close to her crotch, made her jolt awake and throw herself into the corner away from her bed; shaking as the fear that ruled her life constantly since puberty resumed its wicked torment over her. The oldest step brother stood before her, sneering down at her legs as the night shirt had ridden up to her upper thighs. "Mmm that's made my morning. Now stop being a lazy slut and move your fucking arse or I'll give you something to be terrified about!" He stomped out of the room, leaving the door open. She cautiously uncurled from the corner, darting to slam the door shut behind the older step brother. Turning, the wall of mirrors opposite caught her attention. She analysed herself, wondering when she had become 'lazy slut'. The woman gazing back at her was quite petite with a bit of chubbiness which infuriated her to no end. Her shoulder length hair was choppy and jagged. It frequently stuck up at the back, another pet hate for her. Hazel eyes shot with green sparks. Her high, prominent cheek bones made her face look longer and exotic, they showed her strong Cherokee heritage. Her lips formed a perfect bow, a slight natural pout made her seem younger and more carefree. She always felt that where she had extra weight her boobs were unattractive, not perky or firm, she felt the same about her butt. She had love handles and a small belly but nothing about her body said fat to a casual observer who was not cruel, more that she was a full woman with curves. She was slightly shorter than average, making it easier to do gymnastics as being shorter and lighter but strong for their size gave shorter gymnasts an advantage over taller ones in moves such as a cast to a handstand on the uneven bars, something she loved to do. Her feet were slim but highly arched so that she found heels easier to wear as they didn't pull her muscles too tight across her tall arches. This was a plus in gymnastics but a problem for life.

Tears pooled in her already sorrow filled eyes but with a firm mental shake and a soft plea to Mother Nature to guide she quelled such negative thoughts. She was not the 'lazy slut'. She was Luca, a highly skilled gymnast, a new age healer, a survivor. No one and nothing would take that from her. Twenty one years growing up in North Dakota made a girl hard, it was just a bonus her step family was   shit.

Routine took over; Luca went first to the chest of drawers for underwear, then to the closet for skinnies and a turtle neck. The jewellery box was next, a purple crystal on a thin silver chain joined the blue one on a leather thong. Two rings of beautiful Celtic knots went onto her right ring finger. Silver bangles went onto her left wrist. Her jaggedy hair was pulled back into a loose tag at the base of her neck by a simple purple ribbon. Purple crystals braided with silver chains and red feathers went into her ears. Putting on a cheery grin Luca spoke to herself, pep talking her into going downstairs. "Come on girly. Man the fuck up. They can't kill you, you've proved that twice. The step father would not let them try again. The inflictor won't be there. Mum might talk to me. It could be the day she wakes up and smells the curry powder. We could be living carefree and manless by midday, chin up girly. Smile. Smiling fucks them up as they want you depressed. Don't surrender. Don't let them win." Making sure to put a bounce in her step she waltzed out of her room and down the flight of stairs to the floor everyone else slept on. The older step-brother was sprawled on his bed on his back, topless, staring out at her, still sneering. Anyone else might find his toned six-pack attractive or his muscular shoulders gape worthy. But to Luca they just made her throw up a little in her mouth. As his hand moved to the waist of his sweatpants she fled down the corridor to the main staircase where she paused to compose herself, she glanced to the other step's room, his hand was already gripping himself as he leered at her chest. Luca almost fell down the stairs. Bastards. Sick bastards. She couldn't believe it. How could they just lay there with their doors open and do that. How could they do it and look at her. They were her step brothers! With another mental shake, they quickly piled up over the course of the day, she skipped into the kitchen. The step father wasn't up yet, nor was mum. The reason being, they were on holiday, there was no need to get up. Luca sighed and began to cook breakfast, taking care not to let her thoughts wander so nothing was burnt, the pain it would cause wasn't worth retreating into dwelling on her recurring dream. A wolf protector? Really? Luca had obviously read too many stupid trashy fantasy romances, believing that men actually protected women. Men didn't love women; they used, abused, and then tossed away women. Another mental shake and Luca plugged in her headphones, keeping one out she let Alfie Boe's stunning voice over take her. When each pile of meat was cooked correctly she put it in the warming cupboard, cooking till it was jammed full. Only then did she turn her attention towards her own breakfast. Banging and crashing from above her head made her aware that her step brothers were going to be pounding into the kitchen in no time so she hastily sliced and diced some apple, banana and pear before throwing some grapes on top and covering the fruit salad with Greek yogurt. Nabbing a spoon she tried to dive out to the garden to eat in peace but the younger step grabbed her wrist just as she opened the back door. The tranquil wilderness of Duluth was blocked again by the designer oak door as she was dragged back into the kitchen and onto his lap. Staying very still Luca waited for the lewd comment she was certain to come. He ripped off her headphones, and then forced her to give him her bowl. Wrapping his arms around her waist he rubbed his stubble along her neck and shoulder, making her shudder and try to bolt away. With a laugh the elder step brother walked in front of her with a wet tea towel, with a flick he caught her under the chin with the tip, a large red welt appearing immediately. Luca gave up the struggle and closed her eyes, they wanted to torment her and she couldn't fight them off. She only hoped they tired quickly and decided food was more interesting. In her mind she chanted over and over. "I'm a survivor. I'm a healer. I'm a survivor. I'm a healer." Another stinging slap of the tea towel across the tops of her breasts caused her to flinch back into the unyielding chest of the younger step brother. She felt his growing interest in her body as his sweaty hands slipped under her turtle neck, groping upwards as the tea towel whipped across her exposed stomach. The sweaty hands kept creeping higher, the lashes following them. Luca knew this was just the beginning, the teasing stage, and she couldn't help but tremble. Every morning since she had been returned to the family two months ago the step brothers had tried to get her alone to torment her, abusing her body with their hands and whatever else they had to hand, stopping when she wept and begged for them to go away. It amused them that she tried to fight them to start with. It annoyed them when she shut down and ignored their touch. It was better to fight, it made the pain end quicker, but Luca felt herself giving up life a little every day. No matter how loud her brain shouted her positive chant, Luca had begun to accept the fact that death would come for her again, at the hands of her step brothers, or the inflictor, and when it did, Luca decided, she would embrace the oblivion that death offered, sinking into endless sleep with no tormentors able to touch her ever   again.

A distant scream floated through the window as the younger step brother grabbed at her breasts with a painful squeeze. Both of the men froze before the older one turned and walked to the window to peer out.

"Holy fuck. What is going on? Halloween was last week, fucking idiots." He turned to beckon at the younger brother who shoved Luca onto her knees on the tiled floor before strutting to join him.

"Oh god! What is going on? Are those dead people? Is that blood?" The younger step brother's voice rose in octaves till he was shrieking, both of the step brothers backing away from the window with looks of pure panic plastered across their features. The screaming grew louder and louder as it drew nearer. Luca slowly rose, not wanting to draw attention to herself. When she stood fully she could see what the step brothers could see, and she wished she couldn't. Bodies sprawled across the sidewalk and some even hung from windows, blood creating a dark red river flowing down the road towards the great lake that lay beyond the holiday house. A huge crowd of people, mostly in their dressing gowns and slippers, were sprinting past the house, screaming and yelling, acting like a stampeding herd of bison being chased by a mountain lion. The crowds thinned and Luca spotted the proverbial mountain lion. Five giant men in a mixture of combat and riot gear chased the panicking crowd of humans, taking down any who faltered quickly, effectively, and bloodily. One of the soldiers who chased the fleeing civilians skidded to a halt beside the side of the house, his face tilted as though he was sniffing the air. Suddenly his head snapped to allow his piercing brown eyes to lock with Luca's soft green ones. A shiver passed through her; a shiver of recognition.

Tobias froze as the scent reached him, his sensitive nose inhaling the sweet perfume of a free Hu. He skidded and paused to try and trace the source of the scent. It was mingled with fear, but that could be from anyone, all the humans feared them. The next smell that hit him had him snapping to stare straight at the house next to him. An amazing mixture of fresh fruit washed over him as he lost himself in beautiful, deep emerald eyes, framed perfectly by high cheek bones and choppy raven black hair. He sensed the others pass him by but he couldn't move, her eyes showing a damaged soul, calling to him to protect her. He didn't stop to think, his animal instincts took over, with a soft snarl he set off at a run towards his mate, for that was what she was, whether she knew it or not. With an almighty crash he barrelled through the door and into two human men he had not seen before, a growl broke from his clenched jaws when he scented her fear on them both, telling him they had caused it, not him. With no doubts he ripped out the closest one's throat and then disembowelled the second. The tiny woman who smelt so good to Tobi backed away in shock. A shout heralded the arrival of a third man, older than the other two, slightly balding with weight builder muscles. As Tobi turned to take down the new arrival he sensed rather than saw the woman crawl onto the counter behind her, retreating into a corner. After punching through the infected one's skull Tobi heard Damian enter the house. Deciding he could deal with the infected female in the room above Tobi turned back to his fascinating prize, the first free Hu female. She still scented of beautiful fruit tinged with fear but also shock, he could not tell which emotion was his doing. Slowly he approached her, making soothing noises as he spread his hands in a non-threatening pose.

"Hello little one. My, you are scared aren't you? I swear I will not harm you, nor will anyone else, you are very important to us. Trust me. I will tell you everything, all you have to do is trust me my little *winyan wanagi.*" He inched closer to her, worried she would panic or faint, she seemed speechless and confused but her terror was slowly fading, the scent of it was growing weaker. A crunch came from the doorway as Lutron entered through the destroyed door. His mask was off showing his mutated features, the pronounced snout and crazy, wiry ginger hair showing off his spliced DNA. Tobi heard a gasp from behind him and turned to face the cowering woman again.

Luca looked from the soldier who had spoken to her then at the one who just walked in, the new comers face making her gasp with shock. He appeared human yet his facial features resembled an orang-utan. She had tried to scream when the first one had killed her step brothers, she had definitely wanted to scream as her step father's blood had hit her face. But now with this mutant in the kitchen she absolutely needed to scream, and she did. As her voice finally returned she let out a shriek and leapt from the kitchen top to the metal bar above her. After a simple somersault she flipped precariously onto the runway over the kitchen to find the one who had spoken to her already waiting there to support her as she slipped backwards in surprise. He held her tight and ripped off his mask, trying to calm her again with gentle noises. Another of his kind came and began to talk to him as she tried and failed to struggle against his solid yet unpainful grip upon her.

"Kill her; don't toy with her. Although she is hot." The newest creature said.

"Smell the air Damian, she is a free Hu, the first female, perhaps there is hope after all" The one holding her growled in response, the vibrations pulsing against Luca's nipples which responded embarrassingly quickly to the pleasurable sensation.

"Her whole family were carriers and she wasn't? Damn that's going to screw her head up. But I guess it helps that you found her, being the most normal of us all. You had better be taking her back to the heli and getting out of here, the hunt is on. Shame to lose the dog smell of yours though." With a slight smirk the one called Damian left her shivering in the arms of her capture, trying her hardest to understand everything said in a hope it would keep her alive. She peered up at the creature holding her. At first he had seemed like the other attackers, with dark chocolate eyes and wide nose of a primate but when she looked closer she could see that his eyes were more the cheeky, loving eyes of a puppy, his nose, though slightly wide, was not flat on his face and when he unconsciously smiled down at her she caught a glimpse of sharp canines, the tip of two fang softly indenting his lower lip. So, she pondered, there were primate and canine mutant humans running around Duluth massacring humans saying they were carriers but she wasn't. Luca's mind struggled to even begin to comprehend how her life had gone from wanting to die as her step brother's took their pleasure from her to being held in the arms of a stranger, a freak creature stranger, who instead of striking her with incontrollable fear actually made her want to pant, even though it appeared he was the canine. Mental brain shake.

"Are you like, a teenage mutant ninja canine?" She found herself blurting out the stupid, completely un-politically correct question instead of controlling her thoughts. The man peered down at her with amused puzzlement in his eyes, his soft looking lips forming a mind melting smile.

"No little funny firefly. I am not a teenager, or a ninja." He didn't respond to the mutant canine bit and she realised she didn't care; she was just intrigued with the truth. It seemed that time slowed down as they looked at each other, learning the other's features, the images being sketched onto their hearts. Luca felt her arms slip round his waist as she let his gorgeousness wash over her. He was certainly tall, at least six ft. six he towered over Luca. His hair was quite unruly, a springy mass of deep auburn curls he kept cut short. He did have stubble across his jaw, it made him look roguish. His eyes were a soft chocolate, warm and sparkling with life. He had broad shoulders that tamper down to a slim but still well-built waist. There was not an ounce of fat on him, pure toned muscle, but not in a gross over weight lifting way that her step father had been. Her fingers brushed along his hips and instinctively cupped his butt; it was firm and sculptured, just like the rest of his body. She felt him jump at her boldness, vibrating with a low growl, exciting her so her lips parted and she lifted up onto tiptoe to press them against his throat, the highest part she could reach. Under her lips she felt him growl again, almost purring, Luca didn't know the word for a canine purr, she had never been allowed a pet. His arms tighten around her, pulling her up his solid body to attack her lips, forcing her to let his tongue explore her mouth. His growling purr grew and Luca felt herself panting harder as she felt his excitement nestled between their bodies, a thick, hard rod resting across her stomach. Luca knew it was a cliché but at that moment she swore she heard a roaring noise and felt her body grow light and float with pleasure and joy brought to her by the stranger.

Tobi was shocked when the small female kissed his throat, he did not hold back his snarl of excitement, and it seemed to excite her more which played havoc with his senses. He wanted to taste her lips, well he wanted to taste a lot more than just her lips but he had some sanity left to know he shouldn't strip her and lick all over to get her scent imprinted on him. Wait, imprinted? Tobi froze even as she kissed him back, allowing his tongue to dive into her sweet sweet mouth. Imprinting, what was he thinking; she's the first female free Hu! But her taste and her desire overwhelmed all of his senses and he stopped telling himself no and allowed his hands to roam and mould her gorgeous little body into his, loving the feel of her soft moans, especially when they became caused by her feeling his raging hard on. In the tiny part of his brain which was still trying to be logic, Tobi heard the approaching helicopter. He struggled with his conscience, to take the woman to the heli or to ignore them and enjoy her as much as possible. As his radio squawked at him to move outside he knew he couldn't ignore the on mission orders of Damian and the overall orders of Woden; all free Hu's were to be escorted away from the infected city as soon as possible and if any team found a free Hu female then they were high priority to be brought back to the base to prevent them from being found and taken by a carrier. With a grumpy snarl Tobi pulled away from the aroused woman wrapped around him and set her back on her feet to move back a few steps, trying his hardest to calm his breathing, to hide his interest in the female to prevent questions from the pilot, annoying as he was.

Luca felt a blush rising from her chest, up her neck and blazing across her cheeks. She had been wrapped round a total stranger! Maybe the step brothers had been right calling her a slut. She had been eating his face!
"Oh great mother save me from spontaneous combustion because of the shame I feel right now." She sent out a quick, soft prayer to the universe and cast her eyes down to stare at his military clan boots. The roaring she had heard wasn't silly romantic thoughts; it was the helicopter that the other creature had mentioned, Damian or something. Noticing her own feet were bare she

turned to go grab some, assuming he would want her ready to leave. A hand grabbed her already bruised upper arm making her groan.

"Where do you go firefly? We must leave." His rough voice washed through her.

"Shoes, I need shoes. And some personal stuff. Please, just a small bag. I can be done in a few minutes. Please." She tried to hold back the tears of pain, both from her arm and her silly romantic heart.

"Of course, you need things to remind you of home and family. I am sorry for not thinking. I am sorry for your loss." He released her and gestured for her to walk in front of him. Luca retraced her steps of a mere hour ago. When she started up the stairs to the attic she looked back to see the auburn headed man duck in and out of the two step brothers rooms, his face was scrunched up in disgust. He looked confused that she was heading up more stairs and not going into the third bedroom on that floor.

"I wasn't allowed to sleep near my step brothers, they weren't to be trusted." She found herself blurting out. She turned and rushed up the stairs embarrassed, clattering through the door and grabbing her holdall from under the bed. Going to the wardrobe she grabbed her favourite jeans and jumper. Her tops joined them in a pile on the bed along with some undies and socks. A pair of boots. Her jewellery box. The box of dark oak, rattling slightly, went on top. Luca stepped up to carefully remove her dream catcher but a tanned hand beat her to it, gently sweeping the woven crystals and feathers down to rest on the oak box. Avoiding his questioning gaze she started to shove things into her holdall and then filled the rest of the space up with her books. Spiritual ones, romantic one, historical ones and the few books she still had from her grandmother. Looking round her room Luca realised that her whole life fitted into that holdall a bit too well. In fact there was still a significant amount of space left over. Tears threatened to spill over again and she blinked rapidly, forcing them away as she went to fill the space with her second favourite jeans and some more jumpers, she had no idea if they were heading North or South. Pulling on her favourite boots, (the three inch black leather biker ones with purple stitching) and with a sigh that all her clothes were now packed or on her body she zipped up her holdall and tried to hook it over her shoulder. Again the tanned hand got there first, easily tossing it onto his shoulder.

"Be careful of my crystals!" She cried, scared that they had clinked audible. She was shocked that he looked immediately apologetic, shifting the strap gently to allow him to cradle the holdall instead.

"Forgive me *winyan wanagi.* I thought your woven crystals were wrapped in your clothes."

"They are! The loose ones in the oak box aren't!" Luca found herself blurting, an annoying development of being around this man.

"I did not know you had more. I am sorry little firefly. I swear I will protect your crystals with my life." He seemed one hundred per cent serious. And instead of wanting to laugh she felt like kissing him again for being so sweet.

"It's ok, I didn't say, you weren't to know." An awkward silence threatened to descend upon them but the noise of the helicopter was growing and the man gestured for her to precede him again. She went, heading back downstairs. Wanting to avoid the kitchen she stopped in the hallway, hoping he would lead her out the front. But it seemed today her luck was all run out when he went to the back door via the kitchen. Luca felt her boots stick slightly as she tried, and failed, to avoid the pools of blood spreading out from the three bodies. Bodies, not her step family, bodies. Luca kept saying it but their bloodless, staring faces all seemed to scream at her, their eyes following her, blaming her. The smell of fresh cut grass cleaned the air around her as she stepped out into the backyard. Well, backyard is a simple term to describe the huge strip of land that ran all the way down to the lake side. No cost was spared when the step family wanted to go on an outdoors adventure holiday. The view to the lake was broken, however, by a huge Chinook. Luca was proud she remembered some of what her dad had taught her, may he rest in peace now that the step family were dead. The guy took her hand and pulled her towards the lowered ramp. A few meters out Luca stumbled as the powerful downdraft buffeted her. When they got onto the ramp he left her to go talk to the pilot, leaving her to settle into the deep bucket seats that lined the sides of the heli. She chose one near the front, next to a window. The pilot came to help her to strap in, which was good as there were way too many buckles and straps.

"Hey there! I'm Jadar! I'm a mutant cat!" He grinned down at her with his very cat like eyes sparkling with easy humour. His flight helmet kept most of his hair hidden but his eyebrows were a very white blonde. She laughed at his greeting, glad he seemed to be so relaxed. "I will be your pilot this morning. I shall also be the entertainment through these headphones." He plonked them onto her head. "Tobi might be an amazing tracker but his social skills lack! A lot! Anyway he's also old! So he must be boring. I'm eighteen though so way younger and more alive. Wanna go on a date with me?" He asked the question as he concentrated on buckling the straps across her chest, looking straight into her eyes and not trying to brush against her breast more than necessary. Luca knew that, he wasn't a pervert; Jadar seemed much too nice to even consider it.

"I'm Luca, I'll think about it!" Giving her a giant grin and a thumb up that Luca felt compelled to return Jadar strutted, as in full on catwalk hip wriggle strut, back to the cockpit, turning to wink cheekily at her before climbing into his seat. Tobi settled across from her, strapping himself in and placing his headphones on with practiced ease. He seemed to not have heard what Jadar had said to her. Luca was a bit worried about her stuff still she saw it in the netting under his seat; it looked secure so Luca relaxed. She decided to study Tobi, not wanting to think on today as she was scared she might freak out. What sort of name was "Tow-bye"? Deciding that the only way she would learn more would be to ask questions, like her grandmother had always told her to do. But before she could the engines roared and the Chinook shuddered as it took off. Jadar's voice came over the radio, telling someone they were leaving and he would be back after refuelling. Luca looked back as they sped out over Lake Superior at the Leister Park and the golf course her step father had so enjoyed. Jadar's voice entered her thoughts again, chattering away about random things such as the waves on the lake. Luca could see that Tobi's eyes were beginning to close; he looked completely bored at Jadar's nattering.

Tobi let his head drop back onto the head rest, Jadar's mindless chatter washing over him, soothing his raging need to interrogate the heck out of Luca, that or go smack Jadar upside the head for asking her out, geesh he knew she smelt of him, Tobi could smell their combined scents all the way over the other side of the heli! But he couldn't, he had to stay calm, he had to be sensible. He would easily scare her if she saw how different he was to human men, he didn't even know if she had knowledge of human men, the two in her house had seemed interested in her sexually but she had said she didn't trust them and that they were her family. With his eyes closed he found his other senses reaching out towards Luca, her breathing filled his ears, her lingering fear burnt his nose, and he tasted her still raised levels of arousal. Tobi felt his trousers get tighter and tighter as he got harder with excitement, imaging her lithe body trapped under his as he mounted her hard and fast. He growled softly, unable to stop his thoughts.

"How old are you Luca?" He blurted out; glad he asked an innocent question about age and not her sexual experience.

"Well, that's personal!" She blushed before immediately saying, "Twenty one last week but what's it to you?" she was defensive, he could tell, but he was glad she answered him, she knew not to argue with him already.

"Why? It's just your age. I'm probably twenty six; Jadar is like, eighteen or something. So way too young for you to date."

"Well maybe I like younger guys with sexy names! I mean what's a name like Tow-bye mean?" She countered snappily.

"It's short for Tobias, and thanks for thinking my name's sexy Luca!" Jadar piped up.

"Shut it!" Both Tobi and Luca yelled into the mic at the same time, making Jadar laugh at them. Another silence filled the heli, this one more relaxed and friendly, it seemed like they were old friends, a feeling Tobi was used to with the team, but never women, and they were annoying, especially when they tried to join in with the team, mucking up the status quo. Tobi watched as Luca seemed to breathe out, sinking into the embrace of the bucket seat. Her breathing slowed, he guessed it had been a long day for her, and it had only just begun.

Starting and jolting into the harness Luca glowered round the heli, getting her bearings, she had forgotten in her sleep that it had been a drastically eventful morning. She caught Tobi watching her carefully, so she smiled and acted calm. His eyes remained worried though. There was a bump as the Chinook touched down, startling Luca. It was growing dark outside, Luca could see a port and nothing else, no lights were on anywhere, and it scared her.

"Well welcome to New Waterford, Nova Scotia. Here we embark on a wonderfully sleek liner to sail up the coast to merry little Hudson Bay. From there, well we shall let you enjoy some surprises!" Jadar smiled as he walked over to unbuckle her. But before he could reach her he had Luca's holdall thrust carefully into his arms as Tobi stomped towards her and gently started to dismantle the restraints holding Luca down in the chair. His hands did linger against her breasts and crotch, making her flame with passion. He growled softly at her, his teeth indenting his lip sexily as he tried to hold it back, making Luca think him even more sensual. Luca heard Jadar laugh before walking out the door and down the ramp as Tobi looked up from her body and stared hard at her, seeming to wait for something. She raised her hand and brushed against his face, his eyes closed and he vibrated with happiness. They leaned into each other. A loud banging made them start apart as Jadar came back to start unpacking the boxes and crates from the netting in the middle of the heli. Luca felt a blush start as Tobi pulled her up by her hands, steadying her before leading her out, down the ramp and onto the concrete landing area, a large warehouse stood in front of them and Luca heard the sea battering against the sea wall behind the warehouse. The wind swept her hair backwards and she hugged herself, wishing her turtleneck was thicker, or covered in a hoodie, or five. Tobi tugged on her hand again and walked towards the double doors of the warehouse, it seemed deserted, the windows were all broken and there was no light coming from anywhere. She looked worried as Tobi shoved into the door, it didn't open, he rammed his shoulder in to it and it buckled, groaning ominously as it swung open slowly. Tobi rubbed his shoulder and picked up her holdall that was next to the growing pile of crates and boxes Jadar was lugging from the Chinook. Gesturing for her to follow he walked into the darkness beyond the door. They walked to the far end of the warehouse and Luca expected them to end up on the docks to board the boat Jadar had mentioned. Instead a dim light came clear in front of her. A dome like structure had been erected in the middle of the warehouse, it looked plastic to Luca, like the kind of thing that you saw in disaster movies where the infected people where kept. Her steps faltered, causing Tobi to look back at her. His gaze was less passionate now; instead he looked focused, distant, and almost angry. It scared Luca, wondering why he looked at her so.

Tobi felt Luca stop, heard her gasp, but he schooled himself to staying unattached. He smelt the fear and anger of the men inside the dome, the humans who were not carriers, those brought here to await the journey to the base, to safety. Not that they agreed with this. Well, that was not true; some had understood the need, even if they did not comprehend the full reasoning behind it. But human men were violent when in situations they did not understand; they couldn't use their senses to learn more like a creature could. Tobi worried how they would react to Luca; she was small and invoked all his protective instincts. The human men he had found her with had treated her badly, he knew that but did not know how or why. What if all human men reacted the same way, wanting to harm her, they were not known for their protective attitudes towards their women, controlling yes, but true protection, it was rare among humans. Some of the men in the dome were not honourable in the slightest; they were those that ruled the back alleys. Others were the weak and cowardly. It aggravated Tobi more than he could admit that those cruel men were the ones immune to the disease, almost like the Professor was laughing at the irony of his creations. As he and Luca reached the door it hissed slightly, leading to the first compartment of the dome, the waiting area. There were lots of sofa's and seats around a large telly which was showing the film 'Avengers' currently. At the hissing of the door the men on the sofa's turned round and watched him, their eyes darting to Luca as she entered the room. The main group around the telly were instantly hostile, their scents changing to a bitter taste, mixing with their arousal it almost made Tobi gag. On a sofa at the back of the room three men sat together, talking quietly, they all had signs of tears on their faces. Those three he felt sorry for, they had not fought or screamed as they were taken, they had not been with anyone when they were taken, but they seemed to be become friends and this make Tobi hope they were the exception to the rest of the assholes they had taken this time. His attention was pulled back to Luca as she step close behind him, hiding behind his broad back. He growled softly and glared daggers at the group by the telly.

"We have a few hours before the rest of the team's return, those that are here need to start moving through decontamination." He turned to Luca and spoke softly. "This means you have to go shower and scrub off before changing clothes, the clothes your wearing have to be cleaned, we have all the facilities here. All your clothes have to be cleaned in your holdall, so you will have to wear the jumpsuits provided on the other end till your clothes are washed and dried. I can take them to the laundry room as soon as you are in your shower; Jadar is doing it for the men." She nodded, accepting the logic in cleaning everything even though she didn't know what the plague was. "I am worried you might faint, you look so much paler and you shake, would you like one of the men, the quiet men in the corner," he gestured, "to come with you and make sure you are ok, they can wait outside whilst you shower but I want someone to be with you just in case." He was a bit startled he had admitted his worry but she was swaying on her feet, clinging to his waist. She shook her head violently. "But little *winyan wanagi,* you have to understand you need someone to look out for you." She shook her head again and rubbed her head into his chest; he would have thought her feline mix if he didn't have her beautifully sweet human scent wafting from her hair as it moved over his chest.

He almost didn't hear her reply with his blood roaring as it went from his head to his cock rapidly.

"Can't you stay with me? Please, I trust you. Not them. You." Her quiet plea almost brought him to his knees, that or the lack of blood anywhere in his body apart from his newly formed bone straining to be released. He looked down at her face tilted up to his, her fear of men apparent yet she trusted him, a six foot six plus hunk of muscular creature, not man and not beast but a little of both. In his mind that should make her more terrified of him but instead she trusted him, was even attracted to him if the kiss they shared at her house was anything to indicate. How could he deny her, how could he deny her anything when she asked in that soft voice that sounded like a brook trickling over rocks. He gestured to Jadar to come over from moving the crates.

"Jadar, Luca needs a protector, she is weak and scared. You will have to grab her clothes at the same time as the men; she has more clothes so give her her own washer. I know you have to get back to pick the teams up but you can do that after. I can make it an order if it makes you happier." He grinned evilly at him, making Luca laugh against his back. Jadar knew he was joking as well.

"No prob's mate, I need a break anyway. Flying makes my butt numb." He winked at Luca before looking back at Tobi. "If I hit them do I get a bonus?" Jadar laughed and walked over to the men on the sofa. Tobi could hear him hissing at them to make them move towards the men's showers, the three in the corner were already going through the hissing door. Tobi looked down to Luca, waiting for her to make the next move.

Luca looked up at Tobi's expressive face, seeing anger towards the men, respect for Jadar and something else, it was a mixture of attraction, lust, struggled control, and lots of other things she could not interpret passed over his face. Nothing on his face made her worry over her decision, well no more than she was already worried.

"I have to take your bag to the washers, I'll be right back little firefly." He stepped out of her hold, reminding her how weak she was compared to him. She knew what he had said to Jadar but didn't think he meant it so literally. He lifted her holdall and walked quickly away, to the middle door, this one didn't hiss open; Tobi had to yank it hard.

He disappeared inside and Luca felt alone all of a sudden. She wandered over to the kitchen area and pulled open the fridge, her stomach beginning to growl at her, making her smile as she thought of Tobi. The fridge was stocked full of meat. She shut it quickly, the red steaks making her queasy. The next fridge though was perfect for her mood, chocolate mousses and large trifles filled the shelves. She grabbed the strawberry trifle and two spoons and perched on the kitchen counter to munch away, waiting for Tobi to return. She moaned and licked her lips after the first mouthful; she hadn't enjoyed sweet food in what seemed like years. Tobi found her scrapping the pot clean, a look of pure contentment across her face. He stood a few steps in front of her, waiting for her to look up. She did and a sexy flush spreading across her face as she grew embarrassed. She watched as he went to the second fridge and grabbed a chocolate trifle, returning to hop up beside Luca, offering her the pot as he grabbed the discarded second spoon.

Luca was glad he didn't say anything, happy to tuck into the second desert. She noticed that he paused frequently to watch her so she tried to be more controlled, taking small spoonfuls and enjoying each one. They finished the desert together and Luca looked shyly up at Tobi, hoping he didn't judge her harshly for inhaling two deserts. Instead his eyes seemed to glow as he leaned closer. Luca gasped but leant in too, welcoming another kiss from Tobi. But instead of his full soft lips on hers his tongue darted out to brush along her cheek, licking up the smudge of chocolate that she had gotten there. She burst into giggle, as did he, and he hugged her close, licking other parts of her face to clean her. His tongue was rough, not like the stray cats that used to lick her hands but instead softer. When he licked her nose for the sixth time she shoved against is chest crying out,

"Hey! You licked there already so it must be clean! Get off my face, down boy down!" She joked, making him laugh harder at getting caught. He slid of the side and knelt in front of her, still coming up to her stomach, which made her feel very small but protected, not afraid. He snuggled his face into her stomach, tickling her to make her laugh even harder. When he blew a raspberry through her top she shriek and fell on top of him, giggling hard enough that tears began to run down her face. They ended up in a heap, laughing together, their faces close together. Luca felt dizzy with happiness, her life before today seemed distant, her fears washed away by Tobi's teasing antics, it didn't matter to her that he was a huge guy, it should have terrified her but she felt so relaxed.

Tobi was shocked at himself, teasing and playing with Luca to make her smile. But he was also shocked at her, her face became younger and her eyes sparkled with joy. She seemed carefree and at ease, set free almost. When he walked back into the room after putting her clothes in the washer he heard her sighs of pleasure and hurried back to find her enjoying trifle. He smiled to watch her. As he moved closer he noticed a spoon next to her, assuming it was for him he grabbed his favourite trifle from the fridge and joined her. He couldn't work out why he decided to lick her clean, but it felt right, so right. Her laughter was like a bubbling stream, bursting out joyously and catching his happiness to take it to new heights. Being tangled with her made him realise he wasn't just happy to be near her. Embarrassed and worried of scaring her he pulled back a bit, trying to ignore her hurt expression.

"Come little firefly, we do really have to scrub up, Jadar will be wanting your clothes to put the washing on. Follow me little one, come on." He coaxed her to follow him to the third door; this one did hiss open, annoying Tobi that they were designed that way. Inside was like a gym locker room, hooks and benches lined the sterile white room, another hissing door waited at the end of the room, and Tobi knew it would lead to a small camber where the air was filtered before the shower room. This side was much smaller than the men's side that he usually saw. Turning to Luca he saw her sitting on the bench by the door. He held his hand out to her and she took it, still trying to stay distant. He instantly felt guilty for breaking them apart in the kitchen, he knew she wanted him to kiss her but he was not ready to do so again, he had little if any restraint left and knew if he kissed her he really wouldn't stop at that. Swallowing hard he tried to detach himself from what he had to do.

"Sorry little *winyan wanagi,* I know you don't want to but you must undress and go through to the showers, I'll wait here facing the wall, you strip and go through the door at the other end, wait till the air blasts stop then go through and choose a shower, I'll follow when you are through so I do not see you naked so as not to embarrass you." Luca nodded meekly and walked slowly to the end of the room. Tobi turned as soon as he was sure she was starting to undress. The wall was a lot less interesting but he would act with respect and self-control, it was what she probably expected.

Luca kept her sighs at bay as she stumbled to the end nearest the door, furthest from Tobi. She felt drained as if the brief moment of happiness she had shared with Tobi in the kitchen had exhausted her. She was annoyed that he hadn't kissed her but guessed it was because she was plain to him. It was also aggravating that he kept calling her '*winyan wanagi' she* had no idea what it meant, it wasn't her grandmother's Dakota tongue but it was defiantly a Native Indian language and probably a Northern tribe dialect. She made a mental note of looking it up in her grandmother's dictionary and started to strip, sure that Tobi wouldn't spy on her. Carefully folding and placing her clothes on a bench, her boots going underneath she stepped quickly through to the next room, shivering slightly. A loud whirring noise started and suddenly great gusts of cold air blasted her body, cleaning the air around her and buffeting her constantly, the only reason she stayed upright was that the air was blasted from all sides equally. A few minutes passed and Luca was sure she would be permanently deaf by the time they stopped. Just as quickly as they started they cut off, leaving a definite ringing in her ears. Her body felt dry and her hair wildly upright as the door in front of her opened and she almost fell through it. She really craved a shower, to control her hair and to re-energise herself. Righting herself she stumbled out of the air chamber and into the nearest shower stall, it was automatic so came on, jets of warm water, again from all directions, washed over her, powerful enough to make her muscles feel massaged. She sighed loudly now, allowing herself a moment to just let the water washed away everything.

Tobi watched her walk through the door; he waited until he could hear the air jets before he walked slowly over to her neat pile of clothes. She really was neat, tidy and controlled, he thought unhappily, knowing he would probably scare her if he let his instincts take over. But then again, his optimistic thoughts chimed up, she did initiate the kiss, she responded to him a lot, and she seemed to want more from him. She was a little firefly, small and delicate yet with a fire that burnt brightest in the dark. He smiled at this thought and moved to put her clothes and boots in the basket. Tobi took his time undressing as the air chamber was still going. Taking off his boots was such a wonderful feeling, the socks quickly followed them into the basket and Tobi spent a while wriggling his toes and enjoying the freedom off having his feet breath again. He couldn't wait to get back to base so he could spend days barefoot in the woods and meadows. Unbuckling his belt he was glad he had calmed enough to be able to tug his trousers and boxers off. The air was cool on his skin and he quickly stripped off his shirt and top. Standing naked he exhaled and stretched, allowing his back to crack satisfyingly. The air chamber cut off and he moved to put his clothes in the basket and placed it outside the main room, spotting Jadar coming out of the men's side grumbling to himself. Chuckling Tobi walked back in and strode to the next chamber to get filtered in the air chamber. As the vents opened and cold air pummelled his body, making him feel alive. When it shut off he stretched again, clicking more of his body. The next door opened and he was hit by a wall of warm steam. He smiled that she seemed to love hot water to. Stepping out of the air chamber he saw her back to him at the closest shower and couldn't resist. He went to her and hugged her waist, feeling her start in surprise as he put his body flush against hers, holding her hips and he nuzzled against her neck. Her stomach was so soft to touch he couldn't help rubbing his palms across her, causing a soft moan to leave her parted lips. Her head feel back against his chest, offering him her throat and he snarled, pleased at his easy conquest.

Luca sub-consciously heard the door behind her hiss open but didn't expect Tobi's solid body to suddenly rub against her bare back, spooning her where she stood washing out her hair. His hands demanded her attention as the spread across her stomach, his hands easily spanning from hip to hip, his nuzzling and kissing on her neck made her moan shamelessly and she let herself relax into his embrace, tilting her head back for him and arching her hips into his hands. His snarl vibrated through them and she knew she should have felt fear but instead she felt thrilled, the need to move against him growing. She rubbed backwards as his hands separated, one moving up to cup her breast, the other making small circles just above her mound. He skilfully rubbed and pinched her nipple to make it respond to him and it didn't need much coaxing. She moaned again and rubbed back against his chest, feeling his cock stirring as his need grew too. His other hand wandered lower, making her breath hitch as his fingers parted her lips and his thumb made a slow exploration of her female area, making shivers go up and down her spine. He snarled again and suddenly Luca found herself spun to face him. He was kneeling in front of her and before she could make a noise he attacked her with his mouth and hands like he was a desperate man and she was his salvation. His mouth latched around her peaked nipple, ruthlessly sucking her and lapping at her with his tongue, the rough surface making her writhe with pleasure. His hands were also rough with pads of calluses. They ran over her hips and thighs, dipping into her soaked pussy again and again driving her insane with need. She could hardly focus on anything as he moved to the other nipple. When his thumb finally focused on her clit she thought she was dying, her hips bucking hard and before she knew it her body had exploded with pleasure, writhing against Tobi's body as he held her upright with his hand on her hip, pinning her to the wall. Gasping she tugged at his hair, wanting him to stand up and kiss her but he shocked her instead, his face moving down her body quickly to shove it in between her legs causing her to cry out in shock as he forced his shoulders between her thighs, forcing her to basically sit on his shoulders as his tongue replaced his thumb on her clit. Hard, sure strokes across her already swollen clit, making her fall back against the wall, thankful that he was strong enough to hold her upright as she had no strength left in her legs. He feasted on her, relentless, his tongue moving off to flick across her whole pussy, causing her to make strange noises, gasping, and moaning whines. She felt her body start tensing hard, knowing he was going to make her orgasm again. As she clawed his head he thrust his tongue into her and she screamed, cumming hard, feeling him lap at her, drinking from her.

Tobi was crazed with passion, Luca was just so responsive, her body so sweet and as he tasted her juices he almost snarled again, she was just so fucking perfect. Knowing she was wet enough and ready enough he couldn't hold back and quickly stood. He had enough control to know she wouldn't want to be mounted the first time. Wrapping his arms under her thighs he lifted her completely, pressing her back against the wall, he moved her to just above his achingly hard cock. Pausing to make sure her face was still full of pleasure he lowered her onto his tip, growling loudly as her tight little body tried to keep him out but he wouldn't be denied. Pressing harder he saw her eyes close and a loud moan came from her throat, her legs going round his waist to make him give more. Pressing harder and deeper Tobi swore he could see stars, she was so tight and he needed her so much that he could hardly stop himself cumming right then. And he wasn't even halfway in. Growling he pulled out a bit to thrust back in again harder, making them both groan loudly together. He felt her wetness covering him and her pussy stretching to allow him getting further and deeper till he stopped, settled fully in her sweet, tight little body. He was panting hard as was she, her cute little pants fanning across his neck as she clung to him, her body quivering against his. Groaning as he started to move, hard little thrusts staying deep in her, knowing he wouldn't last wrong and needing her to come with him. Luca made soft noises against his throat and claw across his shoulders, her heels digging into his thighs. Knowing he was going as his balls drew up tight he slipped a finger between them and rubbed her clit hard and fast. He felt her blunt little teeth close over his shoulder as she muffled her scream, her muscles clamping around his cock as she orgasmed so hard the world spun. He felt cum shoot out hard of him, covering her insides as he jerked sporadically, her tight perfect body milking him dry till he felt drained, he stumbled back to the wall and slid down it, cradling Luca to his chest as she shuddered, her pleasure drawn out by his cock's twitching and swelling. They were both breathing hard still; their faces pressed into the others neck. Tobi inhaled her scent, unable to stop himself imprinting on it, he knew he was, he knew craving her could be a really, really bad idea but he couldn't stop, she was just so freaking perfect for him. He grumbled unhappily as, a few minutes later his swollen base diminished till she could move away. He loosened his unweilding grip on her, instead of moving though she snuggled closer and Tobi realised she had fallen asleep against his chest, her soft breath tickling his nipple. He sighed and stroked her hair softly, feeling strange, almost surreal. He was just so happy, Luca felt so right, both in his arms and around his cock. Her teeth had marked his shoulder deeply, he could feel the bruise forming, it made him feel something he couldn't describe, and it made him hers. He wished he could mark her the same way but worried he would piece her skin. He knew she would carry his scent for a few days though and that made him pleased. Finally noticing that they were still in the shower with water pouring over them he grumbled to himself and lifted Luca up, managing to stand with her cradled in his arms still; his cock felt cold, missing the tight fist of Luca. Tobi walked to the end of the room, the next door hissing open to reveal a room like the first, each hook had a box under it, fall of clothes. Gently so as not to jostle her Tobi sat between two of the boxes. He brushed a soft kiss on her forehead and Luca stirred, her lips parting to huff cutely, snuggling into him more to deny being awake. It made Tobi's heart stop, her simple actions showing how much she wanting him with her, her trusting nature almost brought him to his knees, she was so wonderful. Not innocent, no, but still perfect, something had happened to make her hardened but she still kept an air of young hope, it warmed him to know she was strong. Stroking her hair he kissed her again and nuzzled her cheek.

"Come on lazy bone, time to wake, we have to get dressed and I need to help Jadar move the stuff onto the boat. Come on my *winyan wanagi.*" With much grumbling Luca sat up, away from his chest and rubbed her eyes sleepily. She started suddenly and almost fell off his lap.

"Oh my god! I am so sorry; I did not mean to sleep. Well I didn't mean to do any of that but oh god I am so sorry. I must be so heavy. Sorry. Let me go its ok I'll move. Sorry." She struggled to stand and Tobi let her, confused by her actions and words.

"You are not heavy, you are perfect. I am glad we did what we did, all of it. Why are you not?" He asked, worried he had done something wrong. Luca didn't look at him as she went to a box across the room and struggled to pull on the clothes. Because it was the females lockers there were underwear and bras, one size fits all it seemed as she pull them on. A t-shirt covered her smooth stomach and bountiful breasts. A jumpsuit covered the rest of her beautiful body; she tied it around her waist and grabbed a jumper to wear instead. Socks and plimsolls went on last. Realising he had to get dressed he moved slowly, in shock, rummaging through the cupboard at the end of the room, grabbing the largest jumpsuit and top in there. He stayed barefoot and stomped through the last door to the communal area on the clean side of the dome, most of the men were already there and Jadar had the first pile of crates through the decontamination process for the crates. Tobi went to help, ignoring Luca completely, his feelings stinging from her rejection.

Luca watched Tobi storm out, feeling embarrassed and hurt. Of course he didn't have a problem with having sex with her, he was male. But she was afraid, she had submitted too easily to him, he was too much, and he spoke the lies the inflictor had. Saying she was beautiful and perfect. Lies to draw her in. She shook her head, ashamed at her weakness, his touch was just so good but that was it, he didn't want her for anything but her body. It was silly of her to think of anything more. She thought of how he let her sleep in his arms, had carried her, had kissed her and woken her gently. He was wonderful. But Luca couldn't trust him, not yet, not this quickly. She ignored her heart that was screaming at her that he was the wolf in her dreams, experience meant she couldn't believe. She trailed after him, out into a room matching the communal room on the other side of the dome. The men were crowded around the telly again, the three loners sitting in a corner talking quietly. Tobi and Jadar were nowhere in sight so she decided to play it safe by joining a group and strolled casually over to the group in the corner. One looked as tall as Tobi but was slimmer, lankier. He had spiked blonde hair and a toned body under his slightly tight t-shirt. Next to him sat a man with stubble and much styled hair. He too was lanky and he wore glasses. The last man was chubbier then the other two, his face open and expressive. The last two had dyed hair of interesting tints. As Luca came close they paused their conversation, making Luca uncomfortable.

"Sorry to interrupt you guys, erm, I just wanted to say hi, and well you seem nicer than them." She gestured behind her at the group around the telly.

All the faces in front of her seemed sad but they smiled slightly at her words. The blonde one on the end patted the space next to him.

"It's ok, we're glad to meet you. I'm Toby, that's Tom and that's Patch, that's what we call him anyway cause of his hair. What's your name? What's your story?" He was friendly but not overly, like he held back. He had gestured at the one with glasses when he said Tom and the one on the end had smiled at being called Patch.

"I'm Luca," she said softly as she sat cautiously, "short for Lucretia. My step family was on holiday in Duluth. They're dead now. That's it really. How about you guys?" Patch spoke first.

"I just worked in a small shop in Duluth, no family, well they're down in Texas but my folks are dead and I'm an only child so it'd only aunts and uncles that I haven't spoken to in years."

"Same basic story for me really." Tom said. "I worked in the museum of Duluth, working in finds preservation and the like, sounds boring but I loved it. Didn't give me much of a social life though. I was there this morning when the big guy who leads this team burst in, grabbed me and chucked me onto the heli along with everyone else." Patch nodded in agreement.

"Yep just grabbed and thrown on the heli, little explanation so kinda confused, been picking up information from that lot but they're just plain rude so staying out of the way for the most part." Toby snorted at Patch's assessment.

"Plain rude? Please, they are scum of the city. They should be dead. I just got off a tour in Iraq, typical, come home and more shit happens in quiet Duluth then in an active war zone. I was on a run when the heli landed next to me, thought it was my team playing a prank but they obviously aren't human so that smashed my plan." Luca was shocked that he was in the army, he didn't look the type but then she probably didn't look like a whore but she felt like one.

"So what have you worked out?" She asked them.
"As far as I know a plague affects most humans and only a small number of us are unaffected. The creatures can smell the plague and are rescuing those not infected to protect us and are killing those that are." The three men gapped at her making her

laugh gently at their faces. Her laugh made them smile.

"Wow you know much more than us Luca." Patch said smiling at her friendly. "We only knew the creatures could smell something different about us. That was it. We were debating wild ideas."

"Well we were. Toby is a bit reserved with his opinions." Tom teased the blonde man. They started bickering like old friends and Luca saw how Toby was actually quite young, all of them were, unlike the group at the telly. The four of them fell into an easy conversation about Patch's and Tom's wild ideas whilst Toby joined in every now and then with logistical errors or just plain logic fails. None of them noticed the time pass or the glares Tobi kept throwing their way. Jadar left to pick up the rest of their team and other teams returned, no other humans came though. The creatures began to carry the crates and boxes out the double doors at the back and one of them came over to them.

"Guessing you're Luca as you're the only female here. Here's your bag and stuff, everything's been washed. The rest of you, all the clothes were placed in carrier bags over there, you'll have to find your own kit." He stomped off and Tom made a face behind his back making them all laugh. Although some of their theories were horrifying the four new friends were keeping a light heart, knowing that they were alive and that they trusted the creatures. As Tom and Patch wandered off to look for their clothes Toby leant over to her and looked at her carefully.

"You don't trust people easily, you've been hurt a lot by people you thought you could trust. Yet you trust the creatures, and you are happy to sit here and talk with us. That means the people who hurt you are dead, or gone. Which is good. But don't trust too easily, there are still evil people here. Tom and Patch? They're safe I think and I'm not going to hurt you. The creatures seem to ignore or respect you; I think they are honourable men so you should be safe with them. But it looks like we're in for a long boat ride, so stay alert, stay away from those men, take care, you're not safe yet." With that warning he walked away and Tom flopped down onto the seat he had just left. He started talking about his museum finds room to her and she listened, very interested in the Native American

Indian artefacts he had. Beginning to think of her grandmother she dug around in her bag and pulled out her dictionary index of the tribes of Northern America. Flicking through she thought of what he said. *Winyan wanagi.* It seemed familiar to her after thinking about it a bit so she went to the North Dakota tribes section. She knew her tribe, the Dakota's were one of three dialects in North Dakota so she looked at the other two, and they seemed similar. Choosing the Lakota tribe first she looked up *Winyan,* it seemed to be in that dialect, meaning spirit or soul. For *Wanagi* the only possible meaning was woman so basically Tobi called Luca his spirit woman. Luca didn't understand what that meant to set it aside, replacing her book. When Tom asked what she was doing she shook her head, brushing it off as nothing.

Tobi growled and lashed out at Dominic, his teasing of Luca's scent driving Tobi insane. He was fed up of the team's disapproval and now their teasing seemed worse. They knew as soon as they got on the heli that he had had sex recently, and the only female near was Luca so they knew it was her scent. Damien was disapproving, he kept telling Tobi how important she was and how she had to stay single and then she would be expected to mate with humans to repopulate their species. Jadar was sulking that Tobi had gotten lucky and not him whilst Lutron didn't say anything. Now Dom was speaking up to tease and rip it out of Tobi for his sullen depression.

"You got laid and now you're a grumpy bastard! What? Did she make you submit to her so you are ashamed?" Dom teased from two seats down in the heli. Tobi heard sniggers over the headset and snarled fiercely.

"Quiet Dom or I will beat you as soon as Jadar lands this thing. I did not submit. I made her scream for me, I took her against the wall and she fainted from the pleasure I forced her to endure. There is nothing to be ashamed of by me, maybe you tease because you are jealous." Tobi's words were slightly garbled as he said it through clenched teeth, a growl building in his throat. Before Dom could reply the Chinook rocked and clunked as Jadar set it down on the strip of the old car park with no warning.

"My bad! We've landed." His amused voice came into Tobi's ear and he let his growl go, enjoying watching Dom's face pale at the obvious threat Tobi offered.

"Enough guys. Tobi knows he was in the wrong but she was willing. That's all that matters, leave it be and let's get down to business. Unpack, decontaminate and help the other teams store everything on the boat, I want to be out of here in an hour." Damian yelled at them. This brought groans from everyone and the subject of Luca was dropped.

An hour later all the boxes and crates had been moved to the boat's hold, the heli's were strapped down on the deck and most of the free Hu's were on the way up the gangway. Jadar had annoyed Damian so he was in charge of sorting out their housing. Tobi spotted Luca hanging back with the three men who had sat on their own. He instantly felt angry at them being near her but managed to only growl a little. He stopped himself going over there to grab her away, his anger growing as he saw none of them offered to carry her holdall. Humans were not gentlemen, he thought with venom. Going against his instincts he turned and stormed up the gangway, stomping to talk to the captain.

"Hey, Jones, I need a favour." Tobi yelled as he walked into the cockpit.

"Sure mate what?" A short primate mix turned smiling; his captain's hat at a jaunty angle, something he thought was roguish. Not that any of the creature females found it so.

"We have a free Hu female. Can she have your cabin so she's separate and safe from the other free Hu's, they're bastards!"

"Sure Tobi, I'll go sort out my shit now so she can move right in. Trey, take over here and get ready to share with me." Jones told the primate next to him as he walked with Tobi to the stairs down below decks.

A rocky ride

A few days of the rocking of the ship and Luca felt like death warmed up. She sat in her pyjamas, hugging her favourite purple crystals as the dream catcher spun above her as the cabin rocked. The crystals were trying to help but the terrible sea sickness was intense, shamefully so. Luca thought it was also loneliness which made her so depressed. People avoided her, she had been too weak to walk to the canteen the last few days so hadn't seen her friends, different creatures brought her food but they didn't stay, her new friends, Tom, Toby and Patch, hadn't visited and it was like Tobi had dropped off the face of the world. Feeling her stomach roll again she dived for the small toilet room that was attached to the cabin and just made it in time to empty her stomach, which amused Luca as she hadn't actually eaten so where the material coming out when she threw up came from was a mystery to her. As she retched dryly on the floor her cabin door opened and the three human men she had so wanted to see wandered in. As soon as they saw how she was Toby was at her side, lifting her up gentle to place her on the bed as Tom ran to grab the medic, Patch fetched her a glass of water. Feeling embarrassed Luca tried to mumble at them, saying it was ok but her throat hurt too much. She reached for the crystals lying on the floor where she had dropped them and Toby passed them to her curiously. Almost immediately Luca felt them warm and start helping her, her throat eased and the tossing in her stomach faded. Briefly she wondered why they hadn't worked the first time she tried but then realized Toby had passed her a purple and a blue crystal, not both purple ones. Cursing herself for a fool she slowly sat up right.

"Whoa Luca take it slow you look like crap." Toby gently held her down by her shoulder as Patch peered at her worriedly.

"I'm ok Toby, really, just sea sick. The crystals you gave me helped, good choice, thank you." She tried to sit up again and Toby let her, staring at the crystals with a little bit of horror in his eyes.

"How do the crystals help Luca?" Patch asked breathily, he too was staring at the crystals worried.

"I'm, well they, erm..." Luca realised she had never had to explain it before, or had people fear her because of her talent. Her step father had known about it already. Deciding to trust the men was hard, but she knew them enough to tell they meant her no harm. "I can heal with the crystals, they react to me and I to them. Some call me a New Age healer, but I believe I use ancient methods that died out as my people, in fact all the Native American people, were overran and changed by the modern world."

"Well that is a handy skill." The medic who walked in said, placing his bag on the floor by her bed and making Toby scoot backwards before he was stepped on. The medic knelt and placed a hand on her forehead. "You are still clammy, and your pulse is erratic." He said checking it at her wrist. "May I see the crystals?" he asked kindly so Luca uncurled her fists and showed him the two crystals, both about two inches long and one inch wide. They were still warm and throbbing slightly; making the medic gasp as he watched them calm and the light within them fade. "You really are a crystal healer." He said with an air of wonder in his voice. A commotion outside Luca's door drew everyone's attention as Tobi pushed Tom aside.

"What's wrong with the female free Hu?" he asked gruffly, not looking at Luca at all.

"Nothing much now Tobi, she healed herself." The medic replied, gesturing to her hands. Tobi looked and grunted, his eyes briefly met Luca's and then he was gone again, not caring to spend another moment in her cabin. "How rude." The medic muttered as he stood. "Well if the crystals help, keep them close, we're maybe half way through our journey. I recommend getting some food and water inside you, little and often to start with, you're showing signs of malnutrition and dehydration. How long have you been ill?"

"How long has the boat been rolling like this?" Luca asked, unsure of the exact time that had passed.

"Five days, today is the sixth. Why? Have you been ill that long?" The medic suddenly seemed more concerned.

"I felt ill as I stepped onto this boat. I had creatures bring me food but I couldn't hold anything down. No one said anything about it being bad, no one has talked to me at all." Luca felt guilty to admit it as her voice caught and tears threaten to pool in her eyes, the medic looked so shocked and angry.

"This is unacceptable. Tobi said you wanted solitude, not isolation!" he growled scarily, his canines showing his species when his face hadn't given much away. "I'll deal with him. You three," he turned quickly on Toby, Patch and Tom, "you care for her, make sure she eats little and regularly and that she drinks at least a litre an hour, if she throws up again, or faints, or anything bad, come get me immediately. Anytime! Day or night!" He swept out of the cabin, leaving silence in his wake as everyone considered his words. Tobi had made sure people didn't spend time with her.

"To punish me." Luca said out loud without realising, making Tom sit next to her on the bed and take one hand; Patch sat on her other side and took her other. Toby knelt in front and it was he that spoke first.

"Luca, why would Tobi want to punish you? What happened between you two?" Before she could deny anything happening Tom squeezed her hand.

"Luca hun, before you lie, remember this. Me and Patch, we're gay, and Toby, he's military. That basically means through one way or another we know something happened. We know it had something to do with Tobi, and we know it went bad. So don't lie, trust us, we can try and help." Patch shuffled uncomfortably about Tom admitting he was gay so freely but Luca had guessed that within minutes of meeting the pair of them. She looked up at Toby and he nodded reassuringly.

"Ok. So Tobi and I got together when we were showering in decontamination. Well we kissed when he caught me in Duluth and then we did it in the shower. It was mind blowing. Only thing is, afterwards I got really embarrassed and ashamed of the way I acted and said that, but he took it as a personal insult that I didn't enjoy what we did and he hasn't spoken to me or acknowledge my existence in any way since." Luca said in all on one breath so the end came out a little gushy but the men around her nodded in understanding.

"So you insulted his manliness by not gushing about how wonderful he was at sex and no he's sulking? Wow I didn't think the high and mighty creatures stooped so low." Tom joked, hugging Luca to his side.

"Really sweetie, he probably thought you were ashamed of having sex with a creature, not that you were ashamed that you had sex with the creature that killed your family." Patch hugged her tight to.

"The guys are right Luca. I think first off we should get food and water into you, then we should set about getting you and he alone together so you can explain to him that the shame was yours not his." Toby was logical in his answer.

"Not there was any shame in your actions, heck if I could get a creature to 'mount' me I so would. Yummy!" Tom giggled before blushing and looked at Patch guiltily.

"Yeah, well. I'm hungry, and so is Luca. So let's go eat." Toby said awkwardly, helping Luca to her feet. "We'll wait outside whilst you dress, can you tie those crystals at your neck of something?"

"Yes, yes I can. Thanks guys, really. Thank you." Luca waited till they were gone to let the tears fall, she was so touched by their friendship and acceptance of her. There was no judgement in their eyes when they spoke of her and Tobi. Sighing at herself and her emotions she quickly washed her face and pulled on her clothes. Simple purple jeans and her baggy off shoulder top with a tiger on the front. Tying the two other crystals to her leather necklace she knotted it on, feeling the crystals warming against her cleavage where they hung. Ignoring her hair in the mirror she brushed her teeth and used mouthwash, it made her feel a bit more human. Opening her cabin door the guys fell in step with her as they led her to the canteen. Luca hadn't been there before so was nervous but it was deserted, lunch was two hours ago and dinner was two hours ahead. The guys led her to the door to the kitchens and they wandered in. There wasn't much activity thankfully and Luca was told to sit whilst Patch made toast, Tom made tea and Toby placed a large glass of water next to her.

"Drink all that before you eat anything. No arguments." His tone left no space for discussion and Luca began to sip the water, wincing as the cold liquid soothed her still slightly sore throat. Soon the water was gone and Toby went to refill it as Tom placed a steaming mug of tea in front of her.

"I had an English boyfriend once, all he drunk was tea so I got good at making it just right. Enjoy!"

Patch came and sat opposite Tom, who was next to her, and placed a stacked basket of toast in the middle of the table along with butter, marmite and raspberry jam.

"Bon appetit!" He announced jokingly, grabbing a slice and swiping butter then marmite over it. He folded it in half and took the biggest bite Luca had ever seen. Grinning happily Patch mumbled something that ended up spraying the table with crumbs, making everyone laugh and dig in, assuming that was what he had meant to say. Luca grabbed the marmite and hoarded it, making Patch mock wrestle her for it. As they were laughing on the floor with Tom and Toby cheering for Patch and Luca respectively, Tobi and the rest of his team stepped into the kitchen.

Tobi absorbed the situation rapidly. Patch was straddling Luca, his face against her neck to protect from her slaps as he put his hands on her rips, too close to her breasts for Tobi's liking. Tom and Toby fell quiet as they noticed the new comers, making Luca's groaning and gasping breaths all the more audible. Before the others could react Tobi had strode forwards and thrown Patch off Luca. He knelt and picked her up before spinning and storming from the room. He heard someone say softly,

"Well that solves the problem of getting the two of them alone." But carried on going. When he reached her room he kicked open the door and deposited her on top of her bed. She had been fighting him but he hadn't noticed.

"Why the hell was that man on top of you? What were you playing at? I ordered you to be left alone in here until I changed my mind, who let you out?" He leant in close to her face as he growled, his voice soft and terrifying. Luca whimpered, afraid of him for the first time, his fangs were fully out and his eyes were nearly black.

"We were just playing, wrestling over the marmite, the medic said I was malnourished and demanded the guys take me to get something to eat whilst he went to yell at you. I know you ordered me segregated and I don't know why." She exclaimed, realising that instead of being afraid she should be angry, Tobi growled at her again, unable to stop himself. She thought it safe to play wrestle with a human man, with others watching her. Yet she felt shame at having sex with him in private. His growls grew in volume as he fought to control his anger. "Stop growling! I did nothing wrong you never let me explain myself!" Luca cried, trying to push him away. As suddenly as he had been on top of her Tobi moved away, causing her to slip from the bed slightly. He breathed hard through his mouth, trying to block her scent from his nose, he was getting aroused by her sweet scent and that was bad, he was angry, not horny damn it!

"Speak then woman, tell me how you intend to explain you apparent disgust at sharing sex with me six days ago."

"There was no disgust for craps sake." Luca had sat up and glared at him, making Tobi pause. "I was ashamed at myself for having sex with you so easily. I believed I had acted just how my step brothers had always labelled me, a slut. I didn't say no, or attempt to slow you down, or even stop to think that you were the one who killed my family. Heck I didn't even care that you're a creature not a human. None of that mattered to me because I wanted you so much. It was only after that I thought about what we had done and I was scared. Scared how you made me feel, how you made me orgasm so much, how different it was to the last time I had sex, how amazing it was, the words you said scared me, I am used to hearing lies of how I look to make me stay with people. I didn't want that to be the case with you. I panicked. I pushed you away. I'm sorry." She stopped and looked at her hands, tears falling softly from her face. Tobi felt instantly guilty, but he couldn't admit he was wrong. Instead he turned and walked away.

Luca sobbed harder as he left, knowing she had screwed it up. Stumbling after him she tried to make it right. She didn't understand his problem. It wasn't that Luca was afraid of him or his masculinity, not at all. She'd been with men, she shuddered at the memories of one particular man, and she liked what happened between men and women. She wanted Tobi, she really did, his sleek movements and muscular body almost drove her mad with desire. It wasn't as if he hadn't made eyes at her. And Luca no longer really minded about the circumstances of her family's death, they would have died anyway and she was glad it was quick. She had said all this to him. So why did he not just bloody well kiss her already. Realising he wouldn't turn back she sighed and made to turn away to return along the corridor to her room to dream what it would be like if Tobi touched her again. A hand on her arm made her pause.

"Why the heavy sigh my firefly?" Tobi was looking down at her with such concerning in his eyes Luca could not stand to ignore the attraction any longer.

"Kiss me Tobi! Damn it kiss me already!" She demanded in a gentle whisper, knowing he would hear. She hadn't expected the light to leap into his eyes or his breathing to increase quite so rapidly.

"Not here, or I shall not stop. I shall take you in the corridor. To your room, now!" He pulled her into his arms and dashed down the hall into her room, bolting the door behind them. Luca barely had time to gasp before his mouth was on hers, his hands tearing at her clothing. Luca tried to help but he had already literally ripped the clothes from her, tossing her onto the bed he started attacking his own clothes, stripping in seconds to stand naked before her. He paused then and looked down at himself.

"This is me Luca, this is all of me. Please, take it." He pleaded with his voice and his eyes. His erection was huge, scaring Luca at first till she reasoned that it had fit once, it would fit again. His body was so damn gorgeous, defined muscle all over his, even his thighs were sexy to Luca. She knew they still had to talk about things, she knew she shouldn't accept him so easily but she couldn't stop herself. Sitting up she opened her arms, thighs and heart to the wonderful creature in front of her. Instead of pouncing like she had expected Tobi fell to his knees in front of her and rested his head on her stomach.

"Thank you my *Winyan wanagi.* Thank you for giving me another chance. I will not fail you again, I do not want you to feel shame, you are not a lowlife person such as a whore, you are a wonderful, kind-hearted soul and they were fools to hurt you with their words so. I swear to you little firefly, I will not be so affronted again, I need you, I shouldn't doubt you. Please, don't send me away ever. Please." He begged her, nuzzling against her stomach, his nose brushing her breasts. She moaned and stroked his head, silently accepting him, all of him, no matter what, for as long as he wanted her. He nuzzled her again and rose slightly to lavish attention on her breasts, making her moan, arch and cling to his hair to hold him there. With little effort he moved her onto her back and wriggled between her thighs. A hand went between their bodies and began playing with her clit, teasingly light on it as he nipped her nipple and then sucked it into her mouth. Luca felt herself moaning loudly but couldn't hold back, his touch was just too much for her senses. Seeming to sense what she needed, he started to rub her clit harder, his other hand drifting lower. Without warning his thick finger penetrated her, making her buck against him and cry out his name.

"So tight, so beautifully tight!" Tobi snarled against her breast before moving up to kiss and lick her throat, his finger thrusts in and out of her hard and his thumb furiously rubbing her clit. "Cum for me baby, cover me in your sweet juice." He demanded and Luca felt something inside her break. Lightening shot through her body from her pussy and neck to everywhere else; she arched of the bed and froze as her orgasm rocked through her body. She felt Tobi removed his hands and his cock nudged her entrance, demanding entry just as Tobi had demanded she cum for him. Luca realised she loved his forcefulness as she cried out again as after a small pause Tobi rammed himself fully into her. He groaned loudly against her neck, the sound and the feel of him drawing out her orgasm till she thought she would cum again just from the sheer pleasure of having him in her again. This time instead of short, hard thrusts Tobi drew almost fully out of her before ramming back in again, his balls slapping against her ass in a way too erotic way Luca thought. He repeated this action, drawing nearly fully out before thrust back deep into her, slowly, driving Luca insane and making her beg him for more, her fingers clawing at his chest. When she thought she couldn't take anymore Luca tensed, her orgasm started but before she could Tobi pulled out full and flipped her over onto her stomach. "Don't move, don't fight and it'll be ok. I need you like this Luca, I really do." Tobi growled, his voice gravelly and sexy as hell making Luca not care how he fucked her. He entered her again from behind, her pussy exploding with pleasure as his thick cock pounded nerves that hadn't been awakened before. Relentlessly he fucked her, his growls mingling with her groans. His hands held her hips in the right place as her upper body collapsed onto the bed where he followed to pin her down gently with his teeth. She started to cry his name over and over as she saw stars and her orgasm burst through her violently, clamping her muscles down around Tobi's cock so he howled and shook as he to orgasmed, ejecting his cum hard into Luca, so hard she could feel it. She also felt his base swell, locking him into her, which startled her slightly. She must have made a sound because Tobi rolled onto his side, still locked in her, and stroked her skin as he kissed her neck and shoulder over and over.

"Sorry, sorry, sorry my Winyan wanagi. I'm sorry I didn't mean to pierce your skin. The swelling will go down soon, I'll leave. I'm sorry." He nuzzled her and went back to kissing and licking her shoulder. Sleepily she turned to look at what he was doing and was mildly surprised to see a bite mark where he was licking; it had stopped bleeding but was very red and looked quite deep. Tobi looked at her so sorrowful that she had to kiss him. It was a long, slow, deep kiss and it was amazing. When Luca broke it off and drew back to look at him again Tobi pulled away and gently withdrew from her body, making her gasp as she was left feeling empty. Before he could leave Luca turned and curled into his chest, kissing his neck and wrapping herself over him.

"Stay Tobias. Please stay. I don't hurt; i'm fine, so please stay." He grumbled but held her tight as she drifted to sleep in his arms again, feeling safe, like she belonged.

The next morning Luca awoke to a soft light spreading across her face, her arm was flung across the bed, the cold, empty dent were Tobi had lain obvious against her sleep warmed skin. She sighed, knowing she had hoped for too much. He hadn't talked to her after the first time, so why did she expect him to do so this time. Holding back the urge to cry she struggled to free herself of the tangle of blankets and stumbled to the shower. The stinging hot blasts of water poured over her, wrenching her to the realm of consciousness fully.

Moving on auto pilot she dried and dressed, her figure hugging clothes making her better about her self-esteem. Tugging on her highest boots she draped herself in silver jewellery and multi-coloured crystals. Feeling prepared and protected she stormed from her room, heading to the canteen to grab breakfast, the night before having depleted most of her energy, her stomach was being very vocal about its empty state. Lost in her angry rant about trusting men, especially half breed men whose baser instincts were prevalent, silly silly woman. Careering round the corner Luca felt like a cartoon "ka'bash!" happened. She found herself knotted with three other people. Staring at the skinny chest in front of her with the strange key hanging from a faded copper chain she knew the men were her friends. She didn't know why but she began to laugh at the situation, finding in highly amusing that she was cursing men and here she was entangled with three of them! They too began chuckling, working to untangle their limbs. The laughing rose and fell as they realised their hair was also caught on buttons and belt buckles. It took a few minutes but finally they managed to be able to sit up, against the walls, facing each other. Patch and Tom had tears in their eyes from tugged hair and sheer amusement, their arms looped around each other to support themselves. Toby was still trying to untangle Luca's hair from his shirt button as the last person Luca wanted to see rounded the corner and froze before them. Tom and Patch started laughing harder at the comical image he presented and it was hard for Luca not to join in. Tobi was juggling a cup of tea, some bagels, and a bowl of butter, a large plate of pancakes, sausages and maple syrup and between his elbows rested a bowl of what looked like trifle. Luca's brain processed this and realised he had gone to get her breakfast as his face went from concentrating cutely with his tongue out to grumpy and hurt puppy like, he turned and walked away, dejected. Luca felt her heart break for him, needing to make him smile care free again. Fumbling to get upright she gasped as she tugged out the remaining hair that was left curled around Toby's button. Over her shoulder she yelled apologies back at the guys as she ran after Tobi with no reason to explain last night or this morning. She caught sight of him ducking through a hatch into a room Luca hadn't seen before, considering she hadn't explored the ship yet she wasn't surprised. She ran in after him and skidded to a halt as she was presented with Jadar's bare behind. Blinking rapidly in surprise she looked round and saw Tobi sat on a bed to her right, the food on the floor beside him. Four more beds were in the room, two on the same side as Tobi and two against the opposite wall. Lockers stood behind each bed and a foot locker at the end of each bed. Lounging on the two beds furthest from the door Luca had come through was the other two creatures she had seen in the house back in Duluth. They were both topless and looked at her with a mixture of shock and disapproval. She started to stutter and back away, her face burning but a wall of solid muscle blocked her retreat. She spun and was only kept upright by the strong grip of the creature behind her, a towering hulk of pure sleek hunter, and his soft eyes drowning her with a strange feline attraction to the tint of his eyes.

"Whoa there little lass." A southern twang came from the scary creature. "Yo so small yo need to be more careful. Too many hulks of creature round here longing for some female attention to be storming everywhere without care. Yo never know whose round tha next corner." A low warning growl was all they got as Luca was ripped from his arms. She found herself bouncing into the bed Tobi had vacated and falling onto the floor on the other side, her breath knocked out of her as fierce roars and howls filled the room as Tobi attacked the newcomer.

"Tobias! Dominic! Heel! Down boys! Behave!" Jadar obviously found the whole fight amazing amusing as the primate crosses came forward. The one called Damian came to assist Luca whilst the scarier orang-utan mix strode straight up to the fighting males and tugged them apart with an arm around each of their necks. They both quickly stop struggling as their oxygen supplies ran out. Damian gently placed Luca onto the middle of the bed as the creature holding Tobi and Dominic turned so they faced her and Damian. Jadar was pulling on low riding jeans and laughing as Damian glared at them all.

"Now. Tobias, explain why you felt the need to attack Dominic. Dominic, be quiet. Lutron let them breathe. Jadar, just no." Tobi shifted, trying to breathe enough to answer.

"She is mine; he should not talk to her! Look at her! Breathe her!" He got louder and angrier with each word, making Lutron tighten around his throat again. Damian didn't say anything and Luca was shocked by the forcefulness of Tobi's statement, she was his.

"Dominic, Tobias claimed her the first night, he was in charge of her care and we all knew he wanted her. He admitted to claiming her not two minutes ago, so why did you scare her and provoke him?" Although his voice was calm his words were cuttingly harsh. Dominic shrugged out of Lutron's hold and stomped forwards to confront Damian.

"He is a fool. She is attractive, more than attractive, she is fucking hot! And that was before I scented her; although his scent is strong hers is still enchanting, even more so considering, ya know, she's in fucking heat!" Luca gasped as they spoke so bluntly about her and her scent, she was sure she had washed thoroughly this morning. Tobi started growling intensely again, making Lutron look worried, well Luca guessed it was worry as it was hard to read his face with his extended snout.

"Dom, stop antagonising him. Dam, punch him already so Tobi stops needing to kill him. And Jadar, I can see you!" Lutron rasped, making Jadar fall backwards in shock after trying to sneak up behind to stick a licked finger into Tobi's ear to 'lighten' the mood. Luca felt her head begin to hurt, all she wanted to do was to grab Tobi and go back to bed, and how had she ended up in a room of males bickering like college girls anyway? Damian seemed to ponder for a moment before nodding to himself, coming to an internal agreement.

"Tobi, chill, when have we not annoyed each other at inappropriate times. Dom, stop being an ass, Tobi has learnt his lesson and Luca is becoming embarrassed. Lutron let him go. Jadar, still just no!" A soft laugh came from everyone in the room at Jadar's defeated and sulky face. Tobi walked over and held a hand out to Luca.

"Come; let us go back to your cabin." Luca took his hand but pulled instead.

"Actually, I really want to eat this food that you got. It's all my favourite breakfast stuff which makes me think either we have a lot in common or you were trying to do an unexpected kind gesture and were bringing me breakfast in bed. Either way, we need to talk about what you saw in the corridor and why you always assume the worse. Also, i want to get to know your friends, team, guy mates, people..." She trailed off embarrassed as Tobi looked confused and the guys laughed at his confusion.

"You want to stay here? With them? After me and Dom just, and Jadar, and well, we're not human. Why trust us being alone with you?"

"Because you're not human. Because you fought to protect me from apparent danger. Because Jadar makes me laugh, something I haven't done in years. Because Tobi, because." Jadar fist pumped the air and earned a cuff to the back of his head from Dom as Damian studied her. Lutron grumbled and returned to his bed, picking up his book and ignoring them all.

"You are a strange human. Maybe that is why the plague avoided you." Damian mused.

"Oh yea, plague. What? And carrier? And free Hu? And what?" Luca asked, now it was her turn to be confessing confusion. Tobi came and sat behind her, snuggling into her neck before settling her against his chest, placing the plates of food on the bed in front of her. Jadar bounced to sit on the foot locker and Damian grabbed a chair from by his bed and dragged it to next to Luca and Tobi. As Tobi started to basically feed Luca, something she found not the slightest bit strange or embarrassing but more intimate and, although Luca was scared to even think it, loving. Damian started to talk.

"The plague is something we do not yet fully understand, but we do know who created it, the same man who created us. Two years ago we came to Canada and learnt of something changing the way the humans around us acted. They were being infected by an air born disease that does not show until months after infection. The carriers mutate to have a hive mind with one purpose, to destroy all those who use oxygen, so everything but plants. They attack animals first and then other humans. So we were attacked first basically because of our mixed genes. But then not all humans become carriers. Only a very few are not compatible with the disease and these few are not attacked. The Hive mind tells them to take all noncarriers, the Free Hu, as we call them. As for us. I'll give you the basics, it's not pretty. Most of us were taken at a young age and had our DNA spliced with animal DNA by the Professor, the man behind this currently fucked up world. When the technique was successful homeless adults were taken and changed, however, the adults were less likely to survive. The children we were grew and learnt how to use our new powers associated with our creature DNA and, after years of being experimented on, we broke free from our cages and fled the Citadel to flee across the ocean to Canada, where we could hide and not be disturbed. The hope is between the creatures and the free Hu the population of humans on Earth could recover after all the carriers are killed. Unfortunately most creature females are unwilling to mate and so unwilling to have children. The free Hu are mostly men, the free Hu females being stolen away before us creatures can secure them. There are five types of creature... kinda. The three most common are primate, canine and feline. A few rare reptiles exist but they were difficult to create and keep alive as they are cold blooded. Then there is amphibian/reptile which with their combined DNA find it easier to absorb heat and survive. We were created as a private army for the Professor as he plotted world domination; there were lots of world domination plans. He sold some of us to allies we think but these of our kind are still missing. About four hundred of us were kept by him and we escaped together. Only one hundred and fifty females were created so it gets... interesting. Our females are small and lethal, not to be messed with. Most of us males and females were placed into small groups of five to ten and made into combat groups. We lived in sectioned cages. There was little privacy which is why when freed the groups stay together. There were only fifty mated pairs allowed, so those that are now free are very independent and yet jealous of those already mated for the happiness they experience. We are a very highly skilled group; one of our number died and was replaced by Jadar a few months before we escaped which is why he is younger. As you may have understood, I am called Damian; I am the captain of this team, a primate mix. I'm also the oldest, so that's why i'm the captain. Dominic is basically the second in command with Tobias, he's feline and a wonder with languages, seriously, a week and he is fluent in any language, he has over fifty already. Lutron is a primate as well but where I am a gorilla mix Lutron is an orang-utan mix, not many of them survive and those that do are ones with extreme feature changes, you should see him making explosives or judging with a glance how much C4 is needed to take down a wall. Jadar, the young, annoying thing over there, is feline like Dom, but like Lutron he too is a bit over mixed, his eyes and ears are significantly different, making him an excellent pilot. Wait till we startle him, he acts like a domestic house cat and hisses with his hair on end!" All the guys laughed as Jadar shuffled uncomfortably, grabbing a bagel to cover it up. Luca was startled to realised most of the food had already gone, Tobi having fed her during the whole explanation by Dam. She was kinda stunned with the whole, creature created from experimenting on children, thing, and the plague that was wiping out humanity. That kind of shit belonged on every television channel and every newspaper headline everywhere in the world! Bar none! Tobi had been gradually hugging her tighter and tighter, hiding behind her back almost. Luca stroked his leg absent minded, not realising how coupley they looked to the others. Whilst she was distracted Jadar grabbed the last bits of food and retreated from the room and Damian stood, patting Tobi on the shoulder before motioning to the other two that it was time to leave them alone. Minutes pasted, almost an hour disappeared before Luca stirred, causing Tobi to turn and curl around her, hiding his face in her lap now.

Tobi was petrified, this morning all he had wanted was to start winning Luca over by bringing her breakfast in bed and then spending the day seducing her in to being his mate. He had started off bad by marking her without permission. But instead of doing the romantic thing they had ended up talking about, death, disease and suffering, she had seen him attack his friend and publicly claim her as his, without her permission. Then she has just sat there, silent, unmoving for an hour, the longest hour in his life it seemed. What could he do to make it up to her? Tobi didn't know but he just hugged her, mentally begging for forgiveness at his heavy handedness of their infantile relationship. He felt her stir and hugged tighter, scared she was going to push him away and run. But instead her hands began stroking him, his hair, his shoulders and back, as though she was soothing him. He glanced up at her, fearful of disapproval or anger or hurt or something but instead the only word that could have described her expression was loving care. She seemed to glow, but then he was bias, and her scent. It was perfect. So soft and sweet and alluring, and wow, now that she was ovulating she smelt like the most tempting desert that had ever existed. He just wanted to bury his face between her thighs and feast on her for a week; he'd die if he didn't taste the source of the sweet aroma soon. Knowing the room was deserted and the door shut he felt assured that taking her would be safe. Gently, giving her time to pull away or say no he nuzzled back into her lap, her jeans helping him to rub across her crotch, making her gasp with sudden awareness. He loved her responses; they were so quick, so sweet, and so gratifyingly cute. His hands gripped her ankles and drew them apart and down, forcing her to lie back and let him do what he wanted. A mild protest pasted Luca's lips but it was more about the teasing and making her wait than anything else. Tobi squeezed her thighs then slid lower to remove her boots and socks, followed swiftly by her jeans. Her underwear gave him pause, they were black and lacy with pink ribbons, something he had never expected. But they were in his way so they had to go, one tug and they snapped off, exposing Luca's smooth pussy for Tobi's exploration. He took longer this time, really wanting to learn every part of her. With slow movements his finger tip traced the seam of her lips and then spread then, the revealed sight making him pant over her, his cock hardening rapidly. He licked his lips, the tip of his tongue brushing across her, making her shudder. The smell of her drove him insane, limiting the control he had. As much as he wanted to explore, he knew if he didn't start eating her soon, he would be unable to hold back at all and he wanted this to be perfect for her. With his fingers holding her open for his mouth he lowered and latched onto her clit, moaning against her as her sweet juice filled his mouth, driving his control to beyond the limit. His hands moved to pin her down as his mouth moved over her, sucking hard, his tongue swiping along her over and over, his need to hear her cute little moans and gasps as her pleasure grew overwhelming him. He growled and pressed hard down onto her clit, making her buck and writhe, her sounds of ecstasy filling the air. With a slight turn of his head and another vibrating growl Tobi brought Luca to a shattering climax, she screamed his name and he felt true bliss; in her taste, in her claiming of him, her recognition that it was he who pleased her so well. Rearing up he attacked his trousers, freeing his pounding hard cock and with no thought he buried himself in her welcoming body, she tensed under him but he couldn't stop himself, his ass clenched and his arms tensed as they braced himself before he began to fuck her so hard he swear he was going to to die from the painful hold she had on him, the intense friction driving him insane. He knew he had hurt and scared her with his violent taking of her but she was driving him mad with need, he couldn't last long and needed to be buried in her when he did cum. His whole body ripple and vibrated with growls and snarls and rapidly Luca's moans mingled with his as his skilled angling of his thrusts made any discomfort fade and give way to unimaginable pleasure. A loud bang echoed through the room but neither of the lovers heard it. Another rocked the bed as the whole boat shuddered for some reason and although it registered on Tobi's mind he quickly forgot it as he felt Luca start to tense and tighten around his cock, her peak nearing rapidly. A smashing sound made him glance at the door with teeth bared, a threatening, lust madden growl ripping from him as Damian hung onto the door and tried his hardest not to look at Luca as she scream and came. Tobi snarled and couldn't stop his own eruptive release, Damian becoming three as the world shook again, in Tobi's mind and literally. Although he wanted nothing more to collapse and cradle Luca until he was hard enough to take her again, so in about two minutes, he knew Damian wouldn't have disturbed their vocal love making if it wasn't urgent. Now the fuck lust was fading, slightly, Tobi noticed the ship was quiet, the engines having been shut off. Reaching between himself and Luca, he had to massage his swollen cock and balls. Forcing himself to painfully de-swell rapidly to withdraw from Luca. She moaned but was already unconscious from his attack, making it less embarrassing for her that they had been watched for the last part. Tobi struggled to rise without letting Damian see Luca's naked body till his captain threw a spare blanket at him to cover her with before rising to fumble with his jeans. Dipping to kiss Luca's brow before leaving he sighed away his anger. Damian turned and walked down the corridor and Tobi followed, nervous as it became apparent that Dam was limping heavily, clutching his left side, his normally pristine combat pants stained with what looked like grease on their dark material but was in fact, Tobi presumed, blood. He grasped Dam by the shoulder and turned him, suddenly scared by the ashen colour of his face.

"Damian, what is going on?" Tobi asked his voice gravelly with concern.

"The carrier we put in the hold to learn more from broke out, well either broke out or was let out by the idiot group of male free Hu's. It's running around the ship attacking anyone it sees. You're woman will be safe, it's avoiding all free Hu's but we need your help to deal with it, it's stronger than expected." For Damian to admit this meant it was serious and Tobi knew that the sooner the carrier was taken out the better for Luca, and not just because he wanted to be back inside her like he needed oxygen to live.

"Got it, you go to the medic bay, I'll go find the team and organise a trap. Where were they last?"

"Scattered, not sure how many got hurt..." Damian slurred and slumped onto Tobi, unconscious from blood loss. Cursing like a sailor Tobi hefted Dam up onto his shoulder and began to jog down the corridor to go down a deck to get to the medic bay, hoping the medic would still be there and not injured, fleeing or dead. Tobi felt wrenched that he was leaving Luca alone, undefended, completely unaware of any danger, he just hoped she slept through this and that the carrier followed previous examples and left all the free Hu's alone until all other creatures were dead. Reaching the staircase Tobi heard sounds of muffled fighting from above and sprinted down the stairs, barely missing slamming into the medic at the bottom.

"Quick, help me with Damian, he has a major wound to his left side, significant blood loss, been out a few minutes maybe." Tobi gasped; surprised to be out of breath when Damian wasn't heavier than what he could normally carry with ease.

"Bring him in and lay him down, I can try to stop the bleeding but things are bad, Tobi, really bad. How did the fucking carrier get out?" The medic asked frantically rushing into the infirmary, collecting all he needed and scrubbing his hands in record time. Tobi dumped Dam on one of the bed unceremoniously and stretched to crack his back before answering.

"Honestly? No idea. I was busy and then Dam was there telling me a carrier had escaped and was wreaking havoc, and then he collapsed. I didn't have time to ask questions or anything."

"Well shit." The medic repeated this over and over as he cut of Damian's shirt and trousers, exposing a nearly foot long slash up his thigh, over his hip and across his belly. Tobi joined in the swearing, trying hard not to gag and to be useful. But as the medic said, all they could do it stitch him up, pump him full of healing drugs and hope that there wasn't any deep wounds or poison in the slash.

Luca started awake with a cry, something was on her feet and she was convinced it was a horrible, creepy spider. But it was worse, a strange man knelt, breathing on her foot, a hand reaching for her ankle, his face sunken, stretched thin over his bones and petrifyingly devoid of emotion, life, a spark of anything. She shriek and yanked her body into a ball, cowering away from him, unable to do more than that as she struggled to comprehend how she had fallen asleep in Tobi's arms after mind blowing sex and was waking up to a skeletal psychopath in the room with her. The man had fallen backwards and a horrible rattle filled the room as he sucked air in and out. Looked at him as a whole Luca saw that his flesh literally hung off him in places, not that it was baggy around his bones. No. It hung in strips like something had clawed it from his bones, the skin flapped like ripped paper, skin and clothes appearing the same, dirty leather colour. Luca found herself wondering how long the carrier had been infected, because that was the only thing she could think this nightmare was, a carrier of the plague Damian had told her about. With this Luca also remembered she was immune to the plague and so maybe this could help her run from the thing. Deciding action was the best thing Luca darted forwarded and, with months of practice under her belt, she dodged the carrier's flailing arms and sprinted towards the stairs at the end of the corridor. Assuming people would be above deck she pounded up the metal stairs, her bare feet shocking her to find she was naked. Cursing but unable to turn back as the carrier was at her heels, moving with unnerving speed considering the state of its body, Luca flung open the door at the top of the stairs and found herself on the wave swept deck. Hearing the carrier closing on her she ran to the nearest container and leapt for the top of it, just managing to hook her fingers over the edge. Using strength she had forgotten she possessed she dragged herself up and onto the roof of the container. Rolling to her front she waited to see if the carrier could follow her, her body shaking violently as the freezing rain and wind attacked her exposed body. Growling and snuffling reached her ears but they didn't remind her of Tobi, or any noises a creature would make, they sounded like evil itself, trying to catch where her scent led to. The carrier seemed not to be able to comprehend that she had fled upwards, convinced she hid within the container itself. It began to attack the doors. Being swept of its feet again and again as wave crashed over the side of the ship, a full storm was blowing, and the ship was tossed willy-nilly amongst the waves. Luca felt her sea sickness returning in full force and struggled to maintain her grip on the railing along the hatch on top of the container. A screeching sound reached her, telling her that the carrier had breached the container and was now underneath her, searching for her. Tobi and Damian had said that carriers left free Hu's alone, that the hunted creatures first, so why was this one hunting her. Luca thought it could be because she had had sex with Tobi a few times now and that this might lead her scent, as the creatures called it, to be mixed up with Tobi's. That or the carrier wanted to fuck her as she was in heat like Dom had suggested, Luca's more pessimistic and sarcastic mind spoke up. Doing the first mental shake of days Luca peered over the edge of the container to see what the carrier was doing, he was nowhere in sight but she started as Dom and Jadar appeared below her carrying knives.

"Hello. Up here!" She whispered and then shouted when they didn't hear her. They jumped and craned their necks to see her, their mouths gawping as they noticed her very naked upper body.

"Luca? What are you doing up there? Naked. It isn't safe!" Dom was the first to call up to her, Jadar seemed unable to do anything but stare at her breasts.

"No shit Sherlock that's why i'm up here, naked." Fear made her sarcastic and she winched, feeling sorry but unable to say anything to apologise. "I got woken up by a freaking zombie thing, which then chased me up here and I hid up here. It went into the container and now..." A raw howl of fury erupted from the throat of the carrier as it leapt from the container onto Dom, his mouth and clawed hands attacking Dom's face and neck. Jadar tried to pull him of, afraid to stab the carrier too much in case he missed and hit Dom instead. As Luca watched, she noticed that there was a bar above the fighting men and a rope on the other side. Without thinking she acted to save her newly acquired friends. Standing she waited till the rolling of the ship went towards the bar and dived for it, hands out stretched. As the cold metal slapped her palms Luca fisted her hands and spun, twisting around the pole a few times to control herself and stopping in a hand stand over the bar she saw the carrier and Dom were directly below her. Letting lose a warning cry of 'hit the deck' she released her hold and spun down, her legs locked. Her feet rammed straight into the carriers chest and he went flying backwards, the ships railing snapping his body in half and then it slid of the deck into the raging waters below. Meanwhile Luca had flown off the pole and wrapped herself around the rope on the other side. She clung there, shaking and crying from shock, until Jadar ran to get Tobi.

A shaken Jadar rushed into the infirmary and skidded to a halt, staring opened mouthed at the prone figure of Damian, lying still with the medic craning over him, looking worried with deep lines across his forehead. Tobi was sure he looked just as worried as he turned to look at Jadar.

"Report Jadar, where's the rest of the team and where's the carrier?" He asked wearily, not sure he wanted the answers.

"Carrier's dead Tobi, snapped in two and washed overboard. Dom's scratched up but will be ok. I need you to come upstairs now though. Now Tobi. Luca was up there." Before Jadar could finish saying her name Tobi had shoved past him and was sprinting full pelt up the three flights of stairs up to the deck, petrified the carrier had harmed Luca, which was why Jadar needed him on deck, maybe she was injured, dying! Tobi burst through the door and froze, spinning round looking for Luca but he could only see Dom crouched on the floor curing in pain as he tried to staunch the bleeding from a particularly nasty neck wound.

"Where is she!" he howled at him, uncaring of his wound in his panic for Luca. A squeak made him look up and his mouth dropped open as he took in the sight of Luca, stark naked, hanging onto a piece of rope fifteen feet of the deck. She was shaking bad and slipping, dangerously close to falling off altogether. The rope was swaying wildly as the ship rose and fell with each swell and trough of wave. "Luca! Luca baby it's ok! It'll be ok. Trust me, I need you to let go and I can catch you. Ok Luca my *Winyan wanagi,* I am here and will never let you be harmed, please. Trust me and let go." He was petrified the rope might snap, or she might slip when the rope whipped wildly near the edge of the ship deck or that he'd miss and her beautiful and fragile body would shatter on the solid metal deck. He didn't know if he had heard him or if she had the ability to react to what he ask. He could only pray that fate wouldn't let him lose his potential mate now, so close to being happy after so long of depressive loneliness. "Ok my firefly, my brave *Winyan wanagi,* on the count of three. One. Two. Three." He had half expected her not to react but when he bellowed three to make sure she heard him, her arms had gone slack and she plummeted straight into his outstretched arms. He felt her body lose all breathe as he fell to his knees to take the impact force, not that she was heavy to him, but because he wasn't prepared and the drop was big enough for momentum to build up. Tobi had no idea what he said to comfort his sobbing love, only that she wrapped around him and clung like a little spider monkey, refusing to let go even when other teams surrounded them, even when they were escorted down to the infirmary with Dom. The medic tried to get her to let go but she clung tighter, scoring Tobi's back with her nails till he told everyone to back off. He was fine, Luca was alive and she needed peace and quiet and sleep. Growling for everyone to move away, he marched away to Luca's cabin and bolted the door behind them. Gentle he laid on his back on the bed, Luca still curled against his chest, her sobs had ceased a while ago but she still hadn't looked up and released his pincer grip.

"My sweet W*inyan wanagi?* We are safe and alone, please, let me see your beautiful eyes, I need to know you're safe and still the woman I want to hug all day every day. Please little firefly, look at me, show me you are ok." He waiting and slowly he felt her body relax against him, her body began to shake and Tobi got scared. Twisting as carefully as he could, he got himself and Luca under the covers of her bed, trying to warm her. Tobi pressed two fingers under her chin and stared into her beautiful hazel eyes; they were blood shot and tired but strong. Her lips trembled but Tobi was sure it was the cold, her small, soft body was frozen next to his and he was glad his temperature ran a few degrees above the average human. As he rubbed her all over to warm her quicker he assessed her body and found that a few bruises were forming on her arms, ribs and legs. He guessed that was from her climb onto the container, Jadar had explained it all to him, to all the teams, as they had crowded on the deck. When Luca was warmer he slipped from the bed to strip before hurriedly returned, curling round her body to hug and cradle her tight, her head resting on his chest. Tobi felt the first sob rack her body as she finally relaxed enough to feel horror, terror and shock for the events of the afternoon. Thinking Tobi could hardly believe it was only just reaching dinner time. He stroked her hair and crooned at her, rocking slightly and kissing her face over and over, unsure if he did it to reassure her or himself.

"I killed a man, a human. He was ill and I killed him." She sobbed gradually, squeezing against Tobi's side harder as she lost herself to her tears.

"Shush my sweet, my little love. Yes, he was ill and you allowed him to be set free from the plague that was destroying him. You saved my friend Luca. You stopped anyone else from being seriously hurt." At this Luca shot up, staring at him in confusion.

"Anyone else? You mean someone was seriously hurt? What? Tobi I could help them, I could heal them. Please, let me try. I need to, to atone for killing that man, even if it was setting him free I did still kill him." She looked so sincere, so angelic like a guardian angel, that Tobi couldn't say no, which made him worry about how he would keep her safe if she wanted to tell him no.

Luca knew Tobi just wanted to rest, wanted them both to rest but now her head had clear and she knew how to earn forgiveness for killing another human she wanted to get moving, get working. She and Tobi dressed in silence, she stole his over shirt though, which made him smile indulgently. Before they left she grabbed her box of crystals and as many of those entwined in her jewellery as possible. Tobi lead her back to the infirmary and now Luca was fully alive she instantly knew that it was Damian lying mortally wounded on the hospital bed at the end of the room. She cursed that she had missed it and shoved through the crowd of concerned creatures to perch on the side of the bed, causing muttering from the crowd behind her. She ignored them and they quieten when Tobi looked at them she guessed. She concentrated on Damian and drew back the blanket covering his chest to reveal the long gauze pad that stretched down his left side, gently peeling it away caused more grumbles but again they quietened quickly. The wound was raw and green tinged, the odour it gave off was almost rotten, it was definitely infected badly and this worried Luca, she had never healed a badly infected wound. Opening her crystal box she poured them out onto his lap and picked each one up in turn, focusing on his wound and the want to heal it, the infection, the deep tissue and skin tissue damage, the muscles and ligament, even the chipped hip bone. The red, purple, blue and green crystals all felt warm to her and she selected those four of differing lengths, the four crystals that hummed the loudest to her. Brushing the rest into the box she handed it backwards and assumed it was Tobi who took it from her. She could hear the medic arguing with someone, it sounded like Jadar. Blanking them out, blanking everything out but the warm, humming of the crystals and the slash down Damian's side. The green hummed the loudest and purest so she picked it up first and ran it gently around the wound but it seemed wrong, the crystal wanted to go into the wound and like a good listener Luca obeyed, slipping the tip of the thin green crystal into the wound. Luca registered briefly a growl from behind her before she was overwhelmed by the surge of power she channelled through herself into the crystal, helping it do it's healing. The rotting smelled faded rapidly and the slash became less red. Surprisingly it was the red crystal that then started vibrating, causing Luca to remove the green crystal and replace it with the slightly smaller red one, which too wanted to go into the wound. This time she felt the deep tissue and bone heal, knitting together to protect the internal organs within again. Then the purple, running up and down his left side the muscles and ligaments were sewn back together. The blue crystal was happy and cheerful as she brushed it over the shrinking slash in his skin until it was only a faint red line that marred Damian's left side. Breathing deeply Luca sat back, not realising she had almost been lying over Damian's chest. Shaking her head she looked up to find all the faces in the room staring opened mouthed at her, some looked fearful but most held great respect for her. Tobi's eyes gleamed with pride. A soft sigh next to her heralded Damian's return to the conscious world, gingerly he sat up before realising there was no pain or tightness where his wound had been. He too stared at Luca.

"Was it your enchanting humming that brought me back from the brink little Luca?" he asked, his voice laden with emotions. She nodded unable to talk as her self-consciousness returned in full force. Damian lent over and engulfed her into a giant bear hug. Well gorilla hug, Luca corrected herself, smiling slightly. She looked at Tobi to make sure he was ok and was shocked to see tears glistening unshed in his wonderful, expressive eyes. Damian released her and she ducked into Tobi's arms to hide from all the looks of the room full of creatures. Chuckling softly at her Tobi moved through the crowd, taking Luca back to their cabin and a night of restful sleep, no funny business, just snuggled sleep.

A whole new home

It took them three more days to reach the port at Hudson Bay; from there it was a two day drive in big army trucks to the forested area where the creature's base was located. Luca sighed in her sleep as she snuggled closer to Tobi's side as they bounced over another bump. Tobi's smiled widened, it had been a permanent feature since Luca had healed Damian, since she hadn't fought him on any decision and had apparently submitted fully to his dominating mate role. He hadn't let her move from his side for the rest of the journey, so the guys were getting to know her quite well, and her them in return. The team treated her like a little sister who pleased Tobi greatly as it meant they had accepted her, and their relationship. But Tobi was also happy that, the more time Luca spent with him, the more she trusted and opened up to him, relaxing in the guy's presence. The only problem had been she had insisted that the three free Hu men she had made friends with also joined their group; although they were friendly enough Tobi was still overly possessive of Luca and wanted to protect her from all humans. He shifted slightly and Luca jerked awake, in tune with him.

"We're almost there little firefly, I hope you like it, the base is growing a lot and getting quite modern the more we learn and the more information and skills the free Hu's bring us. Some of the free Hu's might not like you, but something will be sorted, you'll probably be placed in the female blocks in the co-habitation area for protection and stuff." Tobi trailed off, unhappy at the prospect of not being able to hold Luca in his sleep anymore, it would not be possible, protocol didn't let a female stay with a male unless they were mated, the odd night was ok but permanently, with a mixed species couple, probably not. Life would be hard but he would prove to the boss that he and Luca were meant to be. Tobi's main concern at the moment was that his ex would prove problematic, especially if Luca was in the same dorm as her. But such things only spoilt the time he had left with Luca so he hugged her tighter and punched Dominic playfully on the arm.

"So, you still saying new age healing is crap?" he joked with his feline friend bringing up the annoying topic for Dom about his distrust of new age healing right up to and during Luca's treatment to him, during which Tobi and Jadar had to hold him down as Damian said how much of a baby Dom was being. Afterwards, his skin was barely red with no visible scar at all Dom retracted all doubt, claiming he was cool with it all along, causing much amusement amongst the team. They started a friendly argument which Luca tried to stop as she didn't want Dom embarrassed or Tobi to offend; her heart was so pure, thought Tobi, happiness and contentment being his only emotion at that time. An hour or so of more bouncy off road driving and the truck they were in pulled up next to the one in front driven by Jadar. In front of them was a huge clearing with a large lake at one end. The forest was dense here and ringed the clearing like sentries. Walled of areas spread out below them, they had parked up on a ridge as the rest of the trucks carried onto the depot. Luca looked out and seemed calm, yet Tobi knew from his highly mutated over sensitive canine senses that her heart rate had increased and her scent had changed to a mix of apprehension and subtle terror. Tobi had been very clear, there were a lot of free Hu's there, and a lot of male creatures, and the female creatures weren't the friendliest. Basically there would be no one there in the same technical boat as Luca.

"There are seven sections. The wild areas; for those creatures who do not want or cannot cope with lots of contact with others and so live along or in small packs. Then there are the four areas for the different species to live together. A co-habitation area: for those who enjoy living in friendship groups etc. this is where me and the team live in a large 5 bed house, with a pool! A new area to house all the free Hu's have been set up. They are apartment blocks of about four to eight people. Then there are the communal areas with a learning building with library and classroom style rooms for free Hu's or creatures to teach their particular knowledge. There is also computer cafes, a huge sports centre with a two storey gym, multiple dance rooms, a large gymnasium, fighting rooms and outdoor track and field, a canteen where you can go eat anytime, lots of different foods, a clubhouse were parties are held every Saturday night, a shopping complex with lots of different floors full of departments i.e.. clothes, food, kitchen etc." Tobi rattled off to explain all the different fenced off areas and buildings that spread out below them. Luca nodded and didn't say a thing, her gaze seemed fixed on the co-hab area, like she was searching for her future home and if she could relate it to his house. He rubbed her arm comfortingly and then slid his hand around hers. "Come on, let's walk down together, it's a wonderful clear day." She gladly walked off with him as the team loaded back into the truck and drove off; she wanted to stay with him as much as he wanted to stay with her. They strolled to the edge of the tree line and followed it down off the ridge. They walked slowly, Luca stopping frequently to smell and touch pretty flowers and sometimes she stopped to listen to the wind go through the branches and leaves of certain trees. Tobi didn't understand what separated one from the other, he knew there were different species but Luca seemed to have no favourite species, nor shape or colour, just some attracted her and some didn't. Reaching the floor where the gates to the base were located they had to stroll along the wall to get to the walkers gate.

Tobi held her hand for the whole walk, they didn't talk really and yet it was so perfect, peaceful and intimate, their relationship not just vocal, as Tobi knew. Luca was his *Winyan wanagi,* his spirit woman, his soul mate. Whatever way he looked at it Tobi knew that he had to fight harder than ever before for Luca, cause if he lost her, he wouldn't be able to survive.

As they reached the gate they were met by a creature Luca hadn't met before, and she knew most of the creatures from the ship by sight. This one was a lanky feline male, his hair a strange tan colour, like a lion Luca supposed. Tobi tried hard not to tighten his grip but he never really succeeded. He took a step forward and the male rose an eyebrow.

"You need not protect the first free Hu female so religiously now, she is safe. I am Jadaih, guard of Woden. He has been wanting to meet with the woman since he first heard word of her, why did you not arrive with the rest of your team Tobias?" he asked casually but his veiled threat was even obvious to Luca.

"Luca, wished to walk amongst the trees', I am sure you have heard of her connection to the old ways through new age application. She wished to greet her new home. Also, I am her personal protector, and she is mine, so we wished for time alone after a lengthy trip. The silence of each other's company was a salve for the grating of nerves that happen in closed spaces." Luca was shocked at Tobi's blunt reveal of their relationship, but glad he wasn't going to abandon her now that they had returned to his base. She had been getting more and more fearful of this till her terror overtook her at the sight of the sprawling militaristic style base. Hearing Tobi admit to her that they wouldn't be together on base made her nerves peak even higher. But his challenging statement to Jadaih made Luca hope he would hang around and see her. Jadaih seemed relaxed at Tobi's declaration though, as though he had expected something like it, which if he had heard from the team of their relationship Luca supposed he would have. He gestured them inside and turned to Tobi once the gate clanked shut behind them.

"So, will you allow me to search your woman or will you do it? I cannot take your word on it so one of us will have to, the females are currently striking for some reason, and Starbright seems to be behind it somehow." Jadaih said almost accusingly of Tobi, who shifted unhappily.

"You may search her so there are no protocol breeches, if Woden trusts you then so do I, as long as you keep in mind that she is mine." Tobi turned and kissed her forehead. "Little firefly, you need to be patted down quickly to make sure you carry nothing dangerous. Jadaih has to do it as he is the guardian asked to do so by our leader. You are mine and you are safe." This seemed to be Tobi's way of assuring both of them that what was about to happen was ok. She stroked his cheek with a smile and stepped towards Jadaih, confident it Tobi's trust in him. He directed her to stand in a frozen star jump like in cop series and he efficiently felt her all over, using the back of his hands across her crotch and chest to make it less threatening. Luca couldn't help flinching away slightly but Jadaih didn't say anything or react, putting her at ease again. She could sense Tobi's rigid expression, a silent half snarl directed at the male touching Luca but he had restraint. Jadaih stepped away when he was done and Luca was enveloped in an intense Tobias hug as he rubbed against her. When he let her go Luca noted that Jadaih looked surprised that Tobi had been so physical with her, and how Luca responded to him. But he held his tongue on that matter.

"Thank you for allowing me to search her Tobias. Woden will see you know for your teams report; she is to be taken to house 5 in the co-hab area, with three of our females." Tobi nodded tensely, reaching an arm around her shoulders to guide her outside. Two jeeps were parked outside, one seemed to be for Tobi and Jadaih and the other had a vibrantly cheerful female creature at the wheel, Luca's bag peaking over the top of the back seat. Jadaih walked to the first jeep and left Luca to say goodbye to Tobi. She knew this was going to happen and thought she would be ok with it but now the time was here she wanted to cry and hide against his chest. Never did she think two weeks ago that she would be so heavily reliant on a single man, a huge, scary man at that. But she was.

"Winyan wanagi. Do not be afraid, the female in the jeep is called Starbright, just know, she might mention me, we dated for a while but that has been over for a while, but I wanted you to know that for me it is a long time ago and you are all that matters. After the debriefing if I can I shall visit you, if not, I shall call. All the houses have phones to the others. I am in house 25, so two streets over. But as the first female free Hu access to you might be limited for a time, bear with them, it'll all work out I swear." He kissed her briefly but deeply, igniting her passion before breaking away and striding off to the first jeep, leaping in as Jadaih sped off. Luca looked again at the second jeep and sighed heavily. Typical, an ex-girlfriend to be her roomie. She walked to the idling jeep and clambered ungracefully in, expecting a harsh comment she glanced at Starbright to find a cheery face beaming back at her.

"Sweetheart, you need bigger heels, these jeeps and most of the furniture was built for six footers or more, not us short arses. You can borrow mine till we sort out your credits." Luca felt her mouth drop open but couldn't stop it, this female was very unexpected. Bright red hair couldn't be natural but it suited the primate female, her chocolaty eyes sparkling with glee. But that wasn't the strangest thing, her face, hands; indeed every visible inch of Starbrights flesh was covered with what looked to be soft brown fur. Luca clamped her lips shut and looked forward again, feeling timid and shy. She wanted female friends but she wasn't sure what to expect. But the questions began to overwhelm her as Starbright put the jeep in gear and pulled onto the main road, heading to the area nearest the lake.

"Credits? Luca asked the simplest question first she hoped.

"Didn't Tobi tell you? Damn thought he had the basics in him. Did he mention us?" she asked, the clipped tone of her voice worrying Luca.

"No Tobi didn't mention credits." She finally answered.

"Right so he did mention me. Sorry, I know it must be hard and I don't want you to think anything. He wants a mate, a family, a settled life and I enjoy running around breaking hearts and being free. I don't want Tobi, he's yours!" She stated as though that was that. "We may have been children with no homes, taken and experimented on but now we are independent adults, our main ties are to our team and then there is a tie of respect to our chief, Woden. We are blunt and appreciate blunt questions if you need answers." Luca nodded her understanding and went back to surveying the landscape, the trees and plants sung with old age energy, the thing Luca believed was what she drew on to heal. An awkward silence descended, the rattling of the jeep was the only sound in the quiet road that round off into the forest. Another gate led off from the main area into the co-hab area, neat, yet sizable cottage like houses lined smartly the roads and col-de-sacs that threaded off the main road. Pulling up outside a pretty purple cottage Starbright bounced from the driver's side and Luca realised Starbright really was almost as short as she was, which lessened some of the apprehension Luca felt at being left with her. She grabbed her holdall before Luca could and strutted down the gravel pathway to the front door. It swung open on well-oiled hinges, no locks being evident as Luca stepped through the door. The entrance hall was separated from the kitchen with a half wall bar and counter, and opened fully onto the living room. The open plan shocked Luca, the light shone from every angle and small hanging charms and wind charms hung at every window. The females in the house seemed to be an open minded as Luca was, or so she hoped. The stairs were tucked through a gorgeously quaint little wooden door set in to the wall, the staircase a steep spiral that led up to four bedrooms, all with en-suites. Two had their doors shut and sounds which left little to wonder about what the other two females were doing in there drifted through the thick wooden doors. The door next to the two shut doors was open and soft vanilla wafted out into the corridor. Starbright ignored that room, meaning it was hers, as she flounced to the last door on the corridor. Swinging it open with a grin she ushered Luca inside a lilac bedroom, a huge bed sat in the middle and built in wardrobe made Luca clap her hands excitedly. The door that led to the bathroom was open and Luca was drawn towards it as Starbright flumped down onto the bed to watch her explore. The bathroom was tiled in white, with decorative swirls of purple, forming delicate flowers. The deep tub looked like a perfect place to soak with a good book and glass of rum and coke. The view out of the window in the bathroom and the bedroom looked over the clearing behind the house, not the backyard but the thinned out forest adjacent to it. Looking round the room she met Starbright's gaze with a serious face.

"I have only one complaint." She struggled to keep a straight face as Starbright's grin began to fade. Luca gestured for her to get up and when she did Luca shoved against the bed till it was tucked against the wall. Stepping back Luca dived face first onto the bed and giggled loudly as she bounced a few times before settling into the lovely soft mattress. "Yet, problem solved." She laughed as she turned to grin at Starbright, amused to her shocked face. "Sorry, been a while since I had a proper bed. It had to be done." Starbright broke into laughter as well at the joy that filled Luca's face.

"I like you little female, you'll fit in here. You hungry?" Still chuckling Starbright led the way back downstairs and into the kitchen. As she left the room Luca noted a sturdy lock on the door where there hadn't been any on the other doors.

"Starbright, why is there a lock on my door unlike the others?"

"Cause you're a free Hu, we added it so if you wanted to get away you could, nothing can break through there, not even a creature, I know, I got some guys to test it!"

Luca hopped onto a bar stool as Starbright rummaged around in the cupboards, lining the side around where Luca sat with fresh meat, fresh bread, ripe fruit, rich deserts and a large jelly. Handing her a spoon Starbright gestured for her to dig in. They chatted about not a lot, Luca about her hobbies like healing and gymnastics, Starbright was a good listener and then returned the favour by talking about the base and the creatures.

"Basically to expand on your last question about credits on base I'll lay it out as simply as I can. All things are brought on a credit system with things that are harder to find costing more credits. You qualify for different credits depending on your job etc. and the credits go on to your id tag. So a Creature gets a base 400 credits and Free Hu's get 500, simply because you refugees need more basic things to start with. Then your job gives you add ons. For any job to count towards credit claims you have to do the job for at least 48 hours each week.

So, a member of a team gets an extra 500, a councillor earns 600 credits more. If you are part of education, catering or cleaning, which a few of our species find quite relaxing, gets an extra 400 credits. Doctors, nurses and medics earn 500 credits extra, like a team member, because there's always the risk that those with medical training will get called into combat." Starbright paused, giving Luca the time she needed to process this system and to ask any questions about it. Luca couldn't really think of any questions about it so instead asked,

"So, you went out with Tobi, how do you feel about him now?" She wished she hadn't straight away but she was generally curious, Starbright was a friendly person and she didn't understand why they had split or why Starbright was still so friendly with her.

"Oh he's a right sweetie; you did good catching him Luca." Starbright exclaimed. "Yeah we were together, oh a few weeks after we got out of the labs, he was so sweet and charming and since Dami wouldn't let me out of his sight I got to know the team quite quickly. Damian's my brother, literally, we were taken together but I was younger, it's how I got this fur, all us young'uns, we were babies when we were taken, all ended up with fur or scales as a side effect, especially the females. Kinda cool actually. Well me and Tobi dated and stuff for a few months but I wanted to be free and he wanted to settle and mate and we both agreed I wasn't his mate material. So that's that really. But I think you are mate material, from the gossip I've heard he's already claimed you, like, twice or something which means he's very serious, you are lucky!" Luca was shocked that she was Damian's sister, and was all surprised at how easily Starbright spoke of her and Tobi's relationship. But mostly it was the whole mating thing that confused her.

"Mate? Mating? Claiming? I don't really understand any of that." Luca was embarrassed to admit as Starbrights mouth dropped open.

"But, to be a mate you must have agreed to it. You mean to tell me Tobi claimed you without permission? The bastard I'll go smash his head in for you for tricking you! Cause not telling you is basically no better than tricking you before you argue!" Luca was scared as Starbright bounced up and pounded to the door but her path was stopped by two males and females piling into the kitchen from upstairs.

"Move Starbight we're hungry!"

"Yeah so hungry for stuff."

"Down boy you only just had me for the third time! This female needs food."

"Ooh free Hu. Hi."

"Aww you're so cute and small."

"Starbright where you going?"

Luca was overwhelmed by the unsubtly of the two couples, the males groping the females as they bent and reached to grab more food and cutlery before tucking into the food around Luca, the females giggling happily. Starbright returned to defend Luca but it wasn't needed, the males were more interested in the females and the females wanted food. Luca murmured hi before Starbright erupted into a rant.

"I am going to beat Tobias! You know the one. He went and claimed little Luca here without her permission! She doesn't even comprehend what a mate is for fucks sake!" There were gasps and exclamations of "No!" from the couples as they all stopped eating to stare at both Luca and Starbright. The males rose.

"We'll help beat him for that." The blonde feline growled menacingly, causing Luca to argue.

"Whoa! No need to beat him, I probably already agree with him. I just want to know what it means, I should know what my role is, what i'm post to do for him to be a good mate and stuff..." She trailed off as everyone glared at her, anger in their eyes.

"The fact you think it is you who has to please him to be a good mate shows how he has mistreated you!" the other male snarled, the females nodding. "A mate's sole purpose should be to constantly prove to his female that he is worthy of her, that she chose right to be his. It is his duty to provide for and protect her, to please her and satisfy her every desire. The male should never make his female change or serve; they are too rare and too precious to be manhandled and upset. A good male states his attention, seduces the female and shows her that he is one hundred per cent dedicated to pleasing her whilst holding back his own violent needs. He should ask her if she wishes to mate. She is in control. That you know not of this worries me as I can scent him on you strongly and you scent says thoroughly mated!" He snarled again, the females joining in this time. Luca was baffled; a society where men wanted to please and protect women sounded like a chivalrous medieval novel she enjoyed readying. She knew that human men mostly respect women in some places but the idea was so alien to her. Tobi was supposed to please her, satisfy her. She thought back, actually he always had. With everything, she blushed happily. Seeing that the males were about to leave with Starbright she jumped off the side and ran in front of them.

"Wait! I think he already does that, just hasn't told me ok. So the whole please and satisfy thing. You mean like, getting me my favourite food for breakfast in bed or carrying my bag or well... erm... making me, you know, finish first and repeatedly in the bedroom." She blushed furiously and stared at the floor, unable to meet the creature's eyes. Starbright stepped forward and lifted her face up by her chin to look into her eyes.

"Do you tell the truth?" Luca nodded furiously. "Then yes, he is being a good mate, but he hasn't said the word mate or claim to you?" Luca thought then slowly shook her head, still too embarrassed to speak. "Has he mentioned staying with you permanently or anything?"

"Well he said he wanted to hug me all day every day and he's really cuddly and protective of me and stuff." Luca mumbled, worried she was still getting Tobi in trouble.

"So he has said he wants you there always but hasn't asked your permission yet. I see, maybe it is not as bad as it first appears." Starbright stepped back and Luca looked around at the other four behind her, the males were frowning but the females were giggling quietly. "You see Luca, it seems like most males he's claimed you to his friends and in front of males who potentially might want you for themselves but he's forgotten that you have an opinion as well." At this the two females burst into laughter and the males shifted uncomfortably.

"Sounds very familiar." The pretty brunette female said through her laughter. "I'm Litha, my mate Tunra, the blonde, did pretty much the same thing. We hooked up once free and I let him stay the night, after he assumed because I had let him stay the night that I wanted him every night, got kinda awkward and annoying but he meant well and once he realised I wanted to be asked first things got better real quick. You just need to make Tobi ask you if you want to be his mate. Tonight could be fun." She grinned cheekily. The other female laughed harder, nodding enthusiastically. Starbright chuckled too and turned to the males.

"Ok guys, time to exit, girly planning about to happen. Make sure Tobi doesn't come round and that he goes tonight but don't say anything about us planning or I'll keep you out of this house for a week!" She threatened jokingly as the males groaned and sulked to the front door after kissing their females goodbye. "Now, everyone up to Luca's room. Bring as much food and pop as you can carry!" Starbright cried like a drill sergeant, making everyone jump and rush to do as she said as she giggled hard and ran up the stairs with them trailing her. They piled into Luca's room and sat in a ring on the floor as Starbright started to explain the plan.

"So, Luca, you need to force Tobi to ask you if he can claim you. Best way to do it, tell him to. Funniest way to do it, tease him by ignoring him till he snaps then say, well you never asked to be my mate so I can do what I like. Guaranteed to be fun for you and everyone watching as he blows his top, grabs you and take you to make sure you never think anything but he's your mate again and it'll be official with him saying, you are now my mate, a lot during lots and lots of mind blowing sex!" Starbright and the others laughed as Luca looked shocked that they were so open about it. "So, tonight it's our welcome back party at the clubhouse for all the teams who returned today. Generally it's a night of all out craziness, alcohol, dancing... and a night of one night stands galore. So, we dress you up to look drop dead amazing, take you out, and party with you, he walks in, sees you in the middle of the floor wriggling and dancing and generally looking like a sex icon and from there, well its easy." Starbright nodded confidently. "Now, let's unpack you and see what you could wear for tonight, we have only a few hours to get ready." Things seemed to flash by for Luca as her things were unpacked, her books placed on a small bookcase by the window, her clothes taking up basically no space in the huge wardrobe and everything being neatly put away by her new friends. Litha, the brunette, was kind, talking to Luca about her Native Indian ancestry as she sorted out the books onto the shelving. The other female, Nessa, was a bubbly person with a wicked tongue, making Luca blush with her crude remarks about how she should make Tobi claim her, making the other females laugh. Both Litha and Nessa were feline, their grace apparent. Starbright kept telling Luca to chill, that Nessa was just joking half the time and there was nothing wrong with gossiping between friends. They started to go through Luca's clothes once everything was unpacked. Her turtle necks were instantly ignored as were her baggy tee shirts and full length jeans. They paused over her vest tops but decided none of them were daring enough. Her boots on the other hand got full approval.

"Four inch black biker heels, man woman they are hot you will smoke with awesomeness tonight in these!" Nessa said holding them up to examine them more.

"Ok girls, the boots are good but she needs to actually wear clothes or she'll be claimed by every male before Tobi even gets there!" Starbright told them, shooing them to their rooms to raid their wardrobes as she hurried to hers. In the lull as they left Luca sighed happily, they were such wonderful people. Humming slightly she picked up her dream catcher and reached up to hang it on a conveniently placed nail above her bed, it was a stretch but soon the room was full of colourful flashes as the setting sun glinted on the crystals. In no time the females were back, bundles of clothes in their arms. Most of Litha's were dresses with bold patterns which weren't the most complimentary of Luca. Starbright's clothes were all way too tight. But Nessa's clothes fitted alight, only thing was, Luca's boobs were bigger, something Nessa loudly pointed out to make her blush. Also Luca blushed a lot as most of the clothes of Nessa's were quite short the longest skirt coming to her knees. But the females said this was normal so Luca blushed and dealt with it, enjoying the banter that passed between the three females, who, it seemed, were all that remained of a team that specialised in seduction and assassination, something that didn't actually worry Luca as much as it should do. In the end they decided on leather for Luca, a pair of hot pants because although they were ludicrously short they did prevent people seeing her ass, well they covered her ass, it was very well defined in the skin tight leather. A matching black corset finished of the bad girl look, the ties down the back teasingly offering glimpses of flesh. As long as Luca didn't breathe she thought she'd be alright. It was a mad scramble for everyone to shower and dress, all of them returning to Luca's room to do each other's hair and make-up and quick pre-drink shots that burnt Luca's mouth, throat, and stomach. Hell they just burnt! Luca's short locks were styled in a 'just fucked' look by Nessa and the other's all twisted and pulled their hair up as all of the females had wonderfully long hair. They all had deep make-up on, making them look like ladies of the night. Luca personalised hers with deep purple eye shadow and lipstick. Just before nine they were ready to go and they left the house.

"Wait I have no money or credits!" Luca realised as they strutted in their high heels down the sidewalk.

"No worries, you'll have a tab tonight and when your credit and id get sorted then it'll be taken off then. But honey! Looking like you do if you have to buy a drink our males are going blind!" Litha stated, making the already tipsy females giggle loudly. They had decided to walk as it was a surprisingly warm night and no one had wanted to drive the jeep to the clubhouse. It was probably a half hour walk, creatures joined them as the strutted, most of the males wolf whistling and starring at Luca. They joked and cat called at Litha and Nessa but nothing serious as their mates soon appeared. Starbright bantered back but Luca just blushed and grinned. A group formed around her and Starbright of admirers, offering to buy her a drink and asking to dance with her at some point tonight, Luca nodded at most, not feeling really threatened as she trusted Starbright to look after her and the males all kept their distance, although their eyes underdressed her frequently. When they reached the club after passing through the gate at the entrance to the communal area Luca paused, causing some of the males behind her to teasingly complain and dodge round her. The clubhouse was a huge warehouse, lights and music blaring out as the door was pulled open by Tunra.

"Come on slow coach!" Nessa cried back at her and Luca was swept forwards by the crowd of creatures laughing and joking, excited about the night of dancing ahead. The music was loud and full of bass that pounded through the many speakers. Inside was a wall long bar with about twenty creatures behind it serving the hundreds of creatures and free Hu in the room. A stage at the end was full of bars and cages to dance against and above that was the DJ booth, a free Hu making shout outs and mixing the music like a pro. Being dragged to the bar by Starbright Luca grinned madly at everyone, she loved dancing and the clubhouse was mad cool. Tossing back the two shots of rum and then chugging the weird mixer Starbright brought them both Luca felt the world begin to spin wildly as she let go of everything, her confusion over Tobi, her embarrassment about what the females had made her wear, her fear of men and males. She just let the spinning take over and shoved with Starbright onto the dance floor to meet up with the other girlies and started to dance. She was quickly partnered by a slim feline who grabbed her hips gently and brought her close to bob and weave with her, the music setting the style of dance.

Tobi was sulking, he had wanted to go to Luca straight away when the briefing ended, but it had taken ages to explain everything that had happened and he got a bollocking from Woden about claiming the first free Hu. Then as he was leaving Tunra and his mate, Jind, turned up and dragged him over to theirs to have a pre club BBQ with loads of males in the feline area and now he was dressed in black jeans and shirt leant by Tunra, being dragged out clubbing when all he wanted was to get to Luca. He had been told to lighten up, that the girlies were heading out too but he still couldn't stop growling at Tunra for keeping him away from helping Luca settle in. Entering the clubhouse he instantly scanned for Luca but it was too crowded to see much. Damian hailed him from a table and pointed to the pint of spare cider and he stalked over there to ask if he had seen Luca. Before he could though Dom and Jadar turned up with Lutron in tow and they started talking at once.

"Wow Dam when the heck did Starbright turn out so damn fine?" Jadar asked.

"And the pretty little thing with her, yummy, looks primate too just minus the fur. Think she's been hiding in the primate zone all along?" Dom purred appreciably, looking at the cages on stage. Tobi ignored him, still unable to see Luca at the bar or any other the tables.

"Not a primate, defiantly human." Lutron said softly, making Tobi gasp and spin to stare at the stage. He almost collapsed as he saw what the others were admiring. His Luca. On stage in a cage, with Starbright. He took in what she was wearing and felt himself harden to rock solid in seconds. Leather hot pants and a leather corset, pushing her breasts together and up, offering the soft white globes to be feasted on by every man's eyes. Luca was dancing with Starbright against the cage poles, grinding and dipping, presenting her firm ass to the room. As the music gets heavier with bass and drums she slapped her ass and moaned naughtily, winking at her friend as she and Starbright began to grind together, their bodies entwining in a taunting, erotic manner. To could see the ties that held her lace underwear together peeking out of her hot pants, causing him to growl thinking how many others could see it. Starbright spotted him and the team over Luca's shoulder and laughed, dancing her way to the bar away from Luca who turned wobbly to his direction, lifting her arms into the air and clasping her wrists together and writhing in front of him, offering her body to him as her movements forced her bountiful breasts to rise to the point Tobi could see the tops of her areola peeking out at him. His growl was almost louder than the music, making his team glance at him, their faces all showing lust for what was his. Tobi didn't think as he shoved from the table, through the crowds and up on stage to grab the guy about to dance with Luca and threw him backwards into the crowded dance floor. She looked surprised and this made Tobi growl more, grabbing her and carrying her to a quiet table in the corner.

"Luca what the hell do you think you are doing, exhibiting yourself in front of everyone! How drunk are you?" he asked watching her sway slightly on the seat opposite him.

"Not that much and I can do as I please Tobias, you don't own me." She slurred, angry at him for moving her so fast as her head spun.

"Don't own you! You are mine Luca so don't anger me!" Tobi felt his patience thinning rapidly.

"No, you never claimed me, never asked me anything, never even bothered to fully seduce me in a manner which I noticed as you want me to be yours. You just fucked me Tobias, nothing more." She was definitely angry now, wanting to go back to dancing as Tobi growled loudly.

"How should a guy go about attracting your attention then Lucratia?"

"First by not using my full name, then by buying me a drink!"

"You are already wasted my little firefly."

"Fuck you! If no more drink buying then the guy should dance with me, let me grind against him, feel the music take over. Oh yea, then things would heat up good and proper!" she said with a wink, shocking Tobi. His little *Winyan wanagi* was drunk and flirting with him crudely, dressed like a slut and saying he hadn't seduced her properly. At first Tobi was offended and his angry ran high but watching her and thinking about what she said he realised she was right, he had just taken her then assumed he could keep her. She had wanted kisses but never had she really said she wanted him forever. He had just assumed. Tobi felt like a fool and wanted Luca to want him as much as he wanted her. She was wasted which wasn't a good start but now he was here he could protect her, maybe even persuade her to go home to sleep in off. But till then if she wanted to dance he would, she looked like she was very comfortable dancing and Tobi wanted to experience her lush body pressed against his, moving to the beat of the music. Tugging on her hand Tobi pulled her on to the dance floor, holding her tight against him as she ground into his body with a purr. He growled and bared his teeth to the males around him who laughed good naturedly and made sure not to brush Luca by accident. Luca spun around and planted her ass firmly against his crotch, wriggling and bumping him till he thought he would cum in his pants she was so good. She liked to dance with her arms up so next time she did Tobi shackled her wrists inside one of his hands and pulled them backwards to rest on his shoulder, making her arch sexily, giving him an amazing view down her cleavage. Tobi thought he actually drooled a little for a while, drinking in his gorgeous woman. He wanted to claim her but at the same time he was loath to leave with her so willing to dance erotically against him. He noted Starbright and Dom in a corner, attacking each other's faces and the rest of the team leaving, Jadar with two females on his arms. All this he noted but his attention never really left the woman in his arms, he twirled and dipped her, making her laugh throatily, and his innocent *Winyan wanagi* was a true temptress at heart. Tobi didn't note, however, that growing attention he and Luca were getting from a particular crowd of creatures behind him. They were watching Luca and muttering, judging her. The leader of the group, a slimy toad like amphibian with webbed hands and a large throat decided enough was enough and stomped towards the oblivious pair; shoving Tobi in the back so he fell on top of Luca he barely managed to keep his full weight off her. Tobi was instantly back on his feet, growling menacingly. Dom was at his side immediately, Starbright moving to help Luca rise. Someone at the door yelled for Damian and the rest of the team to get their asses back inside now.

Luca felt her body aching where Tobi's weight had crushed the air out of it; she felt bruised and knew she had cut her hands and knees. Tobi stood in front of her growling at a really ugly creature with weird pudgy eyes and a bulgy throat. Starbright was fussing her, trying to get her to leave but Luca's head span too much as she was still drunk, but it was fast wearing off as she noticed even the music had stopped.

"Get away from my female!" Tobi snarled out at the amphibian and his group.

"She is yours? Really? She seems pretty free with her affection, dancing with everyone and showing every male here that she is available and wanting it. Her outfit is screaming for attention. If she was one man's then he shouldn't let her out like that! Why is she yours, she only got here today. Unless you took advantage of her when she was dealing with having her family killed. My friend here," he gestured to some free Hu's behind him, Luca recognised some of them as those who came with her on to boat from Duluth. "They say that you screwed her right after killing her family, and she like it. Now if that isn't slutty then what is?" The creature sneered at her around Tobi and she felt something snap, she was fed up of people calling her a slut and no one would insult her tonight!

"Oi shut it you ugly toad! I have had it with people calling me slutty and worse! My step family called me that! For years! My mother did fuck all to defend me! The bastards beat me, tried to rape me, and almost killed me repeatedly. The day they died was the fucking best of my life! I could never hate people as kind as the team that saved me from that living hell I was stuck in. But even so I can drink to mourn my mum; she was kind once I guess. But more importantly I can celebrate this new life I have, the new friends I am making, dancing against one or two guys is not slutty and if one of them is my boyfriend and he approves of it then what is a shitty toad to comment!" She finished her rant screaming, not realising she had shoved past Tobi and was shrieking in the creatures face. Stepping back a step she glared at him, waiting for him to comment or apologise but he did neither. He snorted and turned to laugh with his friends, taking her threats as a joke. Luca saw red and as he turned back her fist ploughed into his jaw, cracking it loudly. He fell to the floor sobbing and for a moment no one moved, there wasn't a sound, but then with a yell one of his friends dived at her but collided with Tobi's broad chest. Damian and Lutron joined him, holding back the amphibians as Dom and Starbright stared at her in shock.

"Get her away from here now!" Tobi ordered Jadar and he grabbed her arm, trying to tug her out.

"You still haven't fucking claimed me and even if you did the whole fucking domineering act is getting old really fast! I am a grown woman and you can go fuck a tree for all I care right now." Luca screamed at him and shoved Jadar away. She ran from the bar and her feet took her the right direction to her new home with the girls. As she reached to front door she glanced back to see Tobi pounding down the street towards her, making her panic and sprint for her room. Still freaking out with rage Luca slammed the door and locked it violently, hearing a bang as Tobi hit the other side. The door was made to make sure she was safe from any attack so she knew she was safe from his rage. Pounding to the I-Dock she put on Screaming, her favourite playlist which consisted of Linkin Park, Bullet for my Valentine and Children of Boden. This, more rum she found in the mini fridge tucked under the bathroom sink, chocolate and manic dancing gradually calmed Luca enough so that the eighth time she tripped over the bed corner, the floor was so comfy she decided it was as good a place to sleep as any.

Luca awoke sprawled diagonally across her double bed, sun in her face, dribble caking one side of her face and her hair in horrid dreadlocks which would take hours to wash and comb out. To start with she could not register what had awakened her until she felt the firm and warm hands of Tobi running along her thigh, over her ass and up her back, the head of his gloriously hard cock teasing her entrance and clit with agonisingly soft caresses. Rubbing and moulding her flesh to arouse her from sleep and awaken her body's response to him. As soon as Tobi knew she was conscious enough he pierced her deep, burying himself up to his hilt within Luca's sweet and tight little body. With a scream Luca stretched for him as without a pause Tobi grabbed her by the shoulder and hip and began a vicious assault on her body, driving her insane with pleasure pain. A few hard, deep thrusts later and Luca knew she was close to cumming, a few more slaps of his balls against her as he buried himself over and over again and she could hold off no longer.

"To...To... Tobias!!!" she screamed as her body shattered with the pleasure. Tobi didn't pause at this first victory but shifted his hips slightly to change his thrust's angle so that now every time his head punched into her he hit her g-spot, causing such pleasure to Luca that she moan and gasped and screamed over and over, one orgasm rolling into the other. Tobi played her body like a fine tuned instrument and he was a master. It wasn't until Luca was hoarse and begging for him to end it did he allow himself to lean fully into her back, pinning her down as with a last few savage jerks he clasped her shoulder between his jaws and exploded inside, his seed filling her and seeping out there was so much. With a moan he stilled on top of her, hardly moving as his knot swelled deep inside her, forcing them to stay join. They lay panting hard, their hearts thumping in time.

"So, you think i'm worthy to be your mate yet?" He joked when he had caught his breath, making Luca groan and hide under the pillow. Tobi laughed and pulled out of her, making her groan again. Slapping her ass playfully his dipped and kissed her lower back, right on the cute little dimples that framed her spine. She purred slightly and snuggled down, drifting off. She looked a mess and yet Tobi felt his cock stirring for her again already. Wanting to give her more time to rest he tugged on his boxers and, glancing embarrassed at the broken window he had gotten in by, he unlocked the door and wandered downstairs to get breakfast. In the living room his team and Starbright sat glaring at him on the stairs but he grinned at them, too happy to care about last night. They had won the brawl and he had gotten Luca back in his bed, well her bed but same difference. Humming to himself he stacked up some food on a tray and waited for the kettle to boil to make Luca a mug of tea. He continued to ignore the team and they just silently glared at him. As he made the tea and headed back upstairs he turned.

"I'm gonna make her eat, then i'm gonna fuck her again. You can stay and listen if you really want to but I intend to make her scream and beg so..." He laughed as they all stared with wide eyes before casually striding quickly for the door. Damian shook his head and then shut the door behind him, making Tobi sure that he would pay for this later. Laughing happily he went back to his gorgeous girl. He found her sitting up, trying to tame her hair. Grabbing the empty desk by the wall, dragging it to the side of the bed and plopping all of the food and tea onto it before getting back into bed.

"What are you thinking little firefly? You look a million miles away and troubled." Tobi asked climbing back into her bed and cuddling against her side, unconsciously stroking her stomach. Luca welcomed his heat as she tried to formulate her thoughts into words.

"Well see, what's happening, it's all so sudden and wonderful. It reminds me of the romance novels I love to read. I keep wondering if somewhere a higher being is sitting in the corner of a coffee shop some place, furiously typing her fingers off to plot and write our lives. I feel that she's taking pity on us, giving us this piece of heaven as the world falls apart. But then it scares me because in every good romance something dreadful always happens just when the couple are beginning to realise how deep their feelings for each other are." Luca looks at Tobi to see if he understood her. He wore a sexy confused expression, he brow wrinkled as her thought hard to understand. He slowly nodded at her.

"I have never read one of your books, but I am sure whatever happens the male always saves his mate. I will always save you my Luca. Nothing will harm you and if anything did, I would destroy the people responsible." His treat calmed Luca's thoughts and she sighed happily, ignored the little voice squeaking in her head that she was too comfortable with him making threats. But she ignored the voice and turned onto her side to face Tobi.

"Kiss me Tobi." she whispered. It was the request he had been waiting for and he happily pounced, locking his lips over hers and attacking her mouth, his tongue tangling with hers. His hands moved from her sides to her hips, lifting her body on top of his, grinding against her as he guided her to his achingly hard cock for round two. Her being on top made things a hell of a lot different, he thought as he strained to stay still under her as she slide down on top of him, slowly taking his full length and moaning so sexily over him, arch her back, forcing her luscious breasts forwards and her head dropping backwards as she began to ride him. Tobi grabbed her hips to hold on to something as he swore the world began to rock with her teasingly slow grinds. Gently he lifted her up a little so he could move enough to start thrust into her at the pace he knew they both needed, there couldn't be gentleness in their relationship like now, he had to prove he was worthy, and she had to feel like she had died and gone to heaven. He wanted her to orgasm at least ten times a day, something he knew he could easily make her do, but he wondered if she could take that much pleasure. Her tight body squeezed his cock, milking him till he knew he was going to explode, her cute little gasping moans telling him she was close to.

Moving a hand from her hip to grab the bed instead he slid his other hand between them.

"Hold on, and cum fast and hard." He growled out the warning before he powerful thrusting up in to her, almost pitching her forwards if she hadn't grabbed his shoulders a second before. He mercilessly rubbed her clit, making her pussy get even tighter around her till they were both yelling each other's names, shuddering together as they came hard, Tobi buried deep in her as he jerked with short sharp thrusts, feeling himself shoot hard inside her. He fell back onto the pillows and Luca collapsed on top of him, their breathing raised again as Tobi wriggled happily.

"Really though, how much do I have to take you to the seventh heaven till you admit you're mine?" He laughed cheerfully, watching as Luca bounced against his chest as it moved.

"Oh you know, till you actually ask me? But first, feed me i'm starving!" She joked back, moving onto her elbows to nibble his chin playfully. He wriggled slightly to sit upright and reached for the tray of food.

Simple Bliss

For a few days things were good. Luca and Tobi spent every hour together. He had packed up her things and moved them to his and she was glad. His room was twice as big as hers and his bathroom was amazing with a giant roll top tub which had been plenty roomy for the both of them. Luca blushed thinking back to how washing Tobi's back had led to so much sex, but then, lots of simple things led to sex with the pair of them recently. Looking round the room she sighed though, as happy as she was, she wanted Starbright to chat to, she was still so unsure of all the stuff about the base. Tobi had sorted out her id and said he would take her shopping at one point but as of yet he hadn't. And today he had been yelled out of bed by Damian and taken off training or something. Things just made Luca sigh. After a few more minutes of sighing Luca was sick and tired of herself, letting herself wallowing in self-pity was wasteful. So she went downstairs and tidied. The team were all men, and they were very messy. There were plates and food all over the living room and kitchen, covering every floor. It was simple work to find a bucket and work her way round, putting things in the bucket to carry them to the kitchen and then put them in the dishwasher. She filled it up and there was so much left over she ran a sink of water in the giant double marble trough sink and put the rest in there to soak. Grabbing some bin bags she then went round and cleaned up all the packaging left over, the take out boxes that had been stacked in one corner and these went quickly out to the bin. Going back for round three she plugged in her iPod, deciding some cool English folk was needed to keep her motivated. Next job was all the dirty clothes left all over the floors. Not knowing what belonged to whom she washed it all together and hung it out to dry. It took three washes to do all the clothing left downstairs and in that time the dishwasher finished and Luca finished hand washing everything else. Whilst the last wash was on she hoovered the living room. After hanging out the last of the clothes she mopped the kitchen floor and wandered around the rest of the lower house to make a list of things to do next. Round the corner of the living room that led out onto the deck outside she found a very clean fish tank, it shocked her to see something that clean in a house that a few hours ago looked like a bomb had gone off in a clothes shop next to a take out. Moving closer she gasps as three wonderfully frilly fish swam into view. Their tails were huge and beautiful and Luca lost herself staring at them. It was only the annoying beeping of the washer that snapped her out of her transfixed state. Shaking her head muttering about needing more sleep obviously she tramped back to the kitchen to take the last load out. The yard was a mess as well, leaves left on the ground and in the pool. Tutting she brought the i-dock outside and started to rack up all the leaves into neat piles at the side of the yard by the back fence. The pool she dredged a little but she couldn't stand it so made a note to find out about if there was a pool cleaning service or something. Strolling back in she jumped a foot in the air at Dom and Jadar staring around the living room.

"What did you do?" Jadar gasped in awe

"Tidied, hopè you don't mind, I was bored." Luca twirled her fast growing hair between two fingers nervously, hoping the males weren't going to freak at her for cleaning their home.

"But Luca, we've only been gone four hours, how did you do so much, all the washing and dishes, everything?" Dom stared at her now, making her shift uncomfortably.

"Well, it was easy, I used to do it all the time so no big thing really guys it was kinda fun." Luca tried hard to stop the tears welling up in her eyes but she was so worried they were grumpy at her. Almost immediately as the first tear dripped down her cheek was Dom and Jadar at her side, hugging her tight.

"Oh no little thing! Don't cry. Tobi will kill us." Dom joked, trying to make her smile which Luca did do a little.

"What's wrong precious? We were shocked is all, I'd forgotten we have cream carpets, I thought they were always mouldy grey." Jadar laughed, making Luca wasn't to cuff him but more because he had admitted not ever cleaning than anything else.

"Why did none of you clean, even a little?" She was curious to know but bet she knew the answer.

"Too lazy." Both males shrugged annoyingly, grinning like kids caught with their hands in the cookie jar. Luca slapped them both gently on the arms.

"Hey no fair Luca!" Jadar pretended to fall to the floor in agony.

"Sorry Luca, we'll help keep things clean from now on, please stay and teach us!" Dom joined in the acting, falling to his knees and hugging her calves, making her laugh hard at the pair of them. Lutron looked positively shocked walking in on the two males on the floor and Luca with tears running down her face as she laughed so hard. He too looked slowly round the room in awe and then starred at Luca just the same way Dom and Jadar had.

"You cleaned all this?" He asked. Luca nodded, having difficulty catching her breath after laughing so hard. "Impressive. Come Woden waits." He motioned for her to walk behind him and the other two males sobered up, rising to their feet and falling in behind her, reminding her ominously of an execution party. That thought wiped all traces of a smile off her face. What did the leader of the creatures want with her? The drive to the main building was short. It looked like a block of offices and in a way Luca guessed it was, there were conference rooms and briefing rooms and secretaries and even labs in the huge glass building in front of her. Stumbling over her feet and wishing the guys would have let her change from her scruffy jeans and tee shirt she had been in to clean she followed them through the large automatic doors and towards the lift. Woden's office and penthouse was the top floor, which Luca felt sorry for him for, he could never really leave work. The life doors slide open on the 32nd floor and Luca inhaled, the floors were polished oak, as were the panelling, above that was a deep red wall paper with flowing vine like detail in black. The corridor led to a bright room at the end of it, two doors on either side were shut. In the room at the end a wall of glass made Luca instantly feel vertigo, you could see for miles. The floor was plush cream carpet, all soft and welcoming. There were sofas arranged in a circle in a depression in the middle of the room. At one end sat a breakfast bar filled with food and drink and the other, Luca stopped herself starring, just, at the creature sat behind the large mahogany desk. Luca noted that Jadiah stood behind him and that the males from the team had rapidly left the room but she couldn't tear her eyes away from the creature's pale green ones in front of her. He stood and walked round the desk slowly and Luca realised that he was only a few inches taller than her, maybe five foot nine max. His face was slim, well his whole body was slim and Luca noted his feet were bare. A strange dragging sound made her glance just behind his feet and her mouth fell open at the sight of a tail, like a lizard's tail, trailing behind him. Stammering she looked back up at his face.

"A tail? Really? Wow, so what amphibian has a tail?" She mentally kicked herself for asked that of the leader of the creatures but he smiled and gestured for her to sit on a sofa, when she did he settled opposite her, careful to sit sideways to allow his tail room to move. Only when he was settled did he speak.

"Hello Luca, I am Woden. I am not amphibian but fully reptile, one of the few rare ones that survived captivity. It is why I am in the position I am in, my species of creature are stronger, faster and more agile than most. We were not mixed with one animal but many reptiles so it is probable that I am alligator, Komodo dragon and gecko. I hear that you are quite a vicious feline yourself, getting into a fight on your first night. Tut tut." Luca almost died right then and there, his voice was pure pleasure and it went straight to her crotch, it slide over her body caressing her. Her brain and mouth shouted "Tobias!" and she snapped backwards, embarrassed she had leant into Woden. He was smiling knowingly and it felt like she had passed a test or something. "You are loyal and stay true to Tobias, even when faced by my hypnotic, seduction. I am impressed female."

"Why do you call me female? I am a human." Luca asked, trying very hard to ignore the fact Woden had admitted to trying to seduce her to test her loyalty to Tobi.

"Well, you claim to be a mate to one of my warriors. No mere human could be that so you must be more. You have joined our family fully, so you are a creature, so you are female." He seemed wise beyond his years, his face smooth and gorgeous,

Luca shook herself slightly, realising he might continually test her.

"Oh, ok then." Woden smiled at her and continued to charm her with his voice, eyes, body.

"So Luca, I hear not only have you been starting brawls you have broken housing regulations, living with a team, rather than you allocated female housemates. This is a grave offence I fear. How do I know what your intentions are to my team, or how they are reacting to you, or their intentions to you? You see, I have to care for all of you and I cannot do that without information, and there has been no information from you, making me think you have been hiding things." His voice had dropped to a whisper and Luca was hard pressed to fight the urge to lean in towards him again. "So little Luca, what is it that you hide? Why are you living with one of my teams and not where I placed you? What makes you think you have any choice in these matters?" Luca felt herself tremble with fear as she realised she had been assuming everything would be ok, she hadn't cared that she was supposed to be with Starbright, not Tobi and the team. Her lip trembled and she took deep breathes, holding her crystal necklaces tight to centre herself.

"I live there as a mate, I am a loyal mate and I support my mate. I clean their house and cook for them; I care for them all as they are my mate's family. By caring for them I support them and they can work harder, without having to care for the house or worry about their meals, they can train harder as I feed them good, filling meals. I am a good mate and by the rights of a creature you can not prevent me living with my mate." Shaking still Luca starred bravely into Woden's eyes and saw respect there before he blinked and two lids shut over them, making her start. Nothing was said for a while, an uneasy silence it seemed to Luca. Woden pondered her, his attractive pull lessening it seemed to Luca. Finally, after almost five minutes Woden started to laugh. Jadaih joined in and Luca felt her angry rise, thinking they were laughing at her.

"Well I see why he calls you a firefly Luca, you are a fierce and strong and worthy mate. I am proud you have chosen one of us as a mate and I am glad he is so protective of you, he needs to be with you sharp mouth. Jadaih let him out before he breaks something." Still laughing Jadaih walked to a door behind Woden's desk and unlocked it, allowing a furious Tobi out. He growled and stalked towards Woden, getting between him and Luca in a protective stance. This amused Woden more and he was totally relaxed and calm so Tobi spun to grab Luca instead and cuddled into her, almost crushing her he hugged her to him so tight.

"I am so sorry for the deception my *Winyan wanagi,* Woden forced me into his smelly cupboard because he wanted to test you. He wasn't supposed to scare you so. Or seduce you." He snarled over her head as he sat cradling her on the sofa.

"I am sorry Tobias, I had to make sure she was devoted enough to be a good mate, that and she is very attractive, it makes me hope more women are found to be free Hu's soon so I might find a mate of my own. She is a very good, loyal mate, though I am not sure she should be caring for all of you so, she is so small she should do less."

"I agree, she has only made a few meals and she was told to stay in my room today, so why she has apparently cleaned is beyond me." Tobi turned an accursing face to Luca, making her blush and hug him to relieve some tension.

"It was only a little, I was bored and restless and and...." the rest of the stammered excuse was drowned out as the males laughed hard at her words.

"Does he keep you overly busy then Luca?" Woden asked, chuckling as both Luca and Tobi shifted embarrassed and avoided each other's eyes. "Forgive me, you make me feel alive and carefree again my friends, something that does not happen a lot with this job. You are free to do as you please, I am proud to welcome you to our family Luca, and hope we may celebrate it more when I get a moment, if I start trying to find a time when I am free now it might be in the next two months." He joked, rising to lead them to the elevator. "Take care my friends. Not everyone will be so pleased about our first mixed couple. Oh and Tobias, you are expected to be back at training after the weekend, don't disappoint me you are a worthy warrior, don't get slack." He turned and prowled back to his study, his tail dragging behind him, making Luca think briefly about how annoying it must be to buy clothes and then have to rip them all the time.

Tobi gazed down at his *Winyan wanagi,* so proud of how she had stood up for him, for herself and for their relationship; also that she had called him her mate, a lot. When Woden had told him, through the cupboard door, that he was going to test Luca he had gone mad, bashing against the door until his shoulder felt horribly bruised. He rubbed it absent minded as they rode the lift down to the ground floor, the whole team was waiting, shuffling uncomfortably as Tobi glared at them, sure they had known when they had dragged him and then Luca to Woden that they knew what he intended to do.

"Sorry man." Jadar was the first to apologise, "Forgive me Luca, Woden's the boss and he wanted to be sure both of you were gonna be ok and yeah..." He glanced at the floor and Tobi felt bad for the kid, he was mouthy but he was also caring, his family was the team, like with all of them and it was important anyone joining the family was treated right and would not upset the status quo. The others muttered and grumbled apologies and they all traipsed to their jeep. It took a few minutes to get all six of them into it without squishing Luca or having her unsafe by not being strapped in. Tobi could tell it annoyed her with them all being so protective of her but none of the males could help it, she was small and soft and weak. Tobi's shoulder protested at every corner as it hit Dom's shoulder every time. Luca started looked at him concerned and Tobi tried extra hard to hide his discomfort from her. They soon got home and piled out; it was Friday night so it was chill time. All the males were looked forward to a weekend of beer, pizza and gaming. When they entered the house they all froze though, Lutron, Dom and Jadar having forgotten that Luca had tidied everything. They gaped and she coughed, drawing their attention.

"Well, I was bored, it was a tip, you can say thank you later. However I have to ask, first, how do you clean the pool because I want to swim tomorrow so it had better be done. And secondly, why was the fish tank the only clean thing in your house?" She tapped her foot with her hands on her hips in such a cute yet sexy way that Tobi just stared at her, thinking of all the things he could do with her in the pool, thinking of her in a swimsuit had him achingly hard in seconds.

"The fish is family, that and they had an automatic cleaner filter thing in their tank. The pool, erm yeah we have stuff for that, somewhere." It was Dam that answered, walking further into the living room to look out at the garden. "We can also get rid of those leaves easily." He looked embarrassed, as did all the guys but Tobi about their house and yard being such a shit hole. All the males agreed, Dom, Jadar and Dam heading out to start on the leaves and pool straight away as Lutron headed to the kitchen to start putting together some snacks and ice buckets for beer and ciders for the weekend ahead. Tobi took Luca's hand and started side stepping for the stairs, making her fight not to giggle at his play innocent face. He liked acting like a naughty teenager with her. At the stairs they both ran and dived for his room, slamming the door shut. Tobi grabbed the edge of his dresser and pulled the whole thing in front of the door.

"Now they can't come drag me out for a few hours." He smiled, turning to Luca and licking his lips. "So you want to swim huh, I didn't notice any swimming costume in that bag of yours, so that means naked swimming. I'll have to kill anyone that sees you naked Luca." He growled, teasing her.

"Well then, tomorrow we have to go shopping, we need to stock up the fridge anyway." Luca shrugged, acting nonchalant even as he stalked towards her.

"Strip for me Luca, I want to see your body. I need to see it. Now Luca, I have no patience." He growled but the infuriating minx just giggled and dodged his pounce. Tobi spread out on the bed, undressing quickly to tempt her to him but she stayed at the other side of the room, looking over his body and licking her lips, her eyes blazing with wanton need. He smiled, she was his alright. He stretched more, showing off his muscles and body, knowing she couldn't keep her eyes of his jutting erection. She surprised him them, starting to sway and step towards him, stripping slowly and teasingly, making sure to take her time as she strip teased for him, making him moan out load and start panting. Tobi stayed still despite his need, wanting her to keep dancing for him. She threw her trousers at him and in the seconds it took for his to rip them off his face she had moved to the edge of the bed and quickly straddled him, grinding herself over his cock. He growled at her but she smiled back, lifting her arms above her head to wriggle and sway on top of him, her wet underwear sliding over his head seductively. Tobi feared he might combust at her teasing, growling and begging her to play fair as he struggled not to grab her and throw her down to fuck her. She took pity on him and stood above him to tug down her knickers and then knelt over his straining cock again, unclipping her bra she let her beautiful breasts free. She held his cock at the base and stroked him softly as she guided his head to her entrance and started to thrust down onto him, her tightness making his eyes water and his back arch. She took him fully and paused, lifting her arms above her head again to make her breasts lift erotically before she began to ride him, her breasts bouncing with each thrust, making Tobi struggle to think clearly, his hands moved to her hips but it was just to touch her, she was fully in charge, something Tobi felt should have been an insult of his dominating nature but instead he felt humbled Luca wanted to do this for him. She moved slowly, rotating her hips and moaning, her head tipped back so he got a perfect view if her body. His head was on the pillows as well so he could looked down and see where their bodies joined, it made him ache so much he thought he would cum then and there but he fought it off, knowing Luca wasn't ready and that she was in charge. She sped up her pace, riding him hard, thrust against him deeper. Her moans grew in volume as she leant back to put her hands on his thighs, changing the angle to allow him to hit her g-spot over and over. She whimpered at him to help her finish as he growled and bucked with her, knowing he was going to cum hard any second. He jammed his thumb against her clit and strummed it furiously, making her scream and writhe before suddenly she tensed and froze, her pussy clamping down on his cock as she came violently, forcing his cum from his cock so hard Tobi howled and fell back to the bed half unconscious. She fell to the side, still joined to him and he managed to roll to make it more comfortable, dragging her up his body to cling to her as they both passed out with pleasure overloads coursing through their bodies.

Almost a week later Luca was terrified, stuck in a nightmare she thought she would never have again. He was walking towards her, the inflictor, he was laughing at her trying to escape, trying to turn and run but she couldn't look away, her legs moved her towards him. He smiled his twistedly kind smile and she feel to her knees in front of him, her hands rising to undo his jeans, she was sobbing, in the dream and in the bed, unable to stop herself freeing his cock and starting to lick his head, his hands going to the back of her head to force her to take him deeper, making her choke, she was struggling now, chocking and fighting but he just knelt over her and fucked her face, tearing at her hair. Then the dream changed, she was in a hole, beaten and bleeding, a pool of blood around her. Looked down at her was the inflictor and her step brothers, sneering at her naked, broken body. They were all naked as well and lent over her, moving her body between them to take her all at once in all three of her holes. She was screaming, fighting, crying, clawing and biting any part she could reach. Bucking in half she sat up in the bed and screamed so loud she felt her throat ripping. Tobi was curled round her crying as he tried to calm her, to wake her, his chest, arms and face were scratched and bleeding, shocking Luca. When he realised she was awake he backed off, scared to frighten her more. She sobbed and curled up in the corner of the bed against the wall as the door burst open, the rest of team rushing in in various stages of dress, most just in their boxers. They all had worried, scared expressions on their faces, looking at Tobi's bleeding, scratched face and then Luca, curled in the corner sobbing and they assumed the worst, growling at Tobi threateningly.

"No! No no not him, never him!" Luca screamed through her tears, struggling to look at the males, still caught in the fear of her nightmare. "It wasn't him, it could never be him." She sobbed harder, ashamed that she had made his friends think he had hurt her, ashamed she couldn't control herself or her fear. Damian looked worried at Tobi and motioned for the other males to leave. Luca could tell they were gesturing at each other, Tobi telling him that he didn't know, she had been dreaming and then attacked him. Damian asked what he could do and Luca felt Tobi shrug, the duvet still covering them both. She tried to control the sobbing but the inflictor's face was there, always there waiting to torture her as soon as she was away from her crystals. Looking up she realised her dream catcher was by the window, not the bed so it wasn't as effective anymore. Shaking she huddled closer in on herself, hearing the door close as Damian left them alone.

"Sweet little *Winyan wanagi,* please, trust me, I need you in my arms, nothing else, no talking, just please let me hold you to help you be safe, you know I will always keep you safe, please let me keep you safe." He sounded so pathetic and worried Luca sobbed harder and could only put out her hand to him, unable to uncurl. He crawled closer so slowly it made her even sadder. She squeezed his hand and he curled around her as much as he could against the wall, trying hard not to trap her but he held her tight and safe in his warm arms. He didn't talk, her sobs lessened and she knew as much as it hurt she had to explain; she had to tell her mate what tortured her so much.

"My step father was an ass, he met my mum when i was sixteen and they were married in a year. When the step brothers and him moved in it was instantly awkward. They kept looking at me. My step father wanted to control me and well I always fought him, he was an ass and I hated him, treating me like dirt just cause I wasn't his, his children got everything but me, I was too old to be brought by sweets and teddies so he tried to make me submissive by beating me. He would always say 'this is the best way, be glad I don't teach you like your mother, this is the best way' as he used his belt to rip open welts on my back. One day I must have pushed him too far because he dragged me by the hair into the closet in their room and handcuffed me to the railing, leaving the door open enough he then went to get my mum. I could hear her say no since she was working but he dragged her like he had dragged me. He threw her to the bed, cuffed her hands and then... well he..." a tear slipped from Luca's eye as she shuddered, trying not to be sick at the memories. "When he was done my mum was bruised and bloody and yet for some reason she looked at him like he was a god. That's what I meant in the club when I said she had been nice once, but since meeting him she was fucked out of her brain, my step-father used to fuck her so much my mum lost her mind with pleasure pain and stayed with him so it would never end. I thought she was weak, I ran away to the streets. By now my step-brothers were in their early twenties, I had a feeling they knew exactly what their father did as they treated my mum like shit and they themselves had tried it on with me a few times. I learnt how to hit pretty quick and my gymnastics helped me climb away from them. When I got on the streets I was cold and depressed all the time, I tried to get jobs in café's but after a few days one of my co-workers always reported me to the police to get the reward my step-father had put out on me. After a few weeks of this a really amazingly hot guy..." Luca felt Tobi tense at this so she rushed on, "... turned up outside my hidey hole and said he knew who I was and wanted to help me stay safe, his name was Danny. By now I was so desperate I believed him and he took me to his flat. I didn't know till almost a year later when he left me half dead on my step-fathers porch after collected a briefcase fully of money that he was a friend of my step-brothers and that my step-father had hired him to teach me a lesson I'd never forget. For weeks after getting home I would wake up screaming from nightmares, my step family just laughing at me. One day I found a crystal in the garden and it felt so smooth and cool I rubbed it against my forehead and then put it under my pillow for safe keeping. That night the dreams weren't so vivid, for some reason I knew it was the crystal so for the next couple of days I searched out more crystals that felt the same as the first and wove them into a dream catcher, before long the dreams had stopped altogether. Other crystals I had found felt different to I experimented with them. I had a stash under my bed. When my step-father realised the nightmares had stopped he invited Danny and my step-brothers to remind me who I belonged to, I ended up so near to death they left me on my floor and went to get bin bags for my body. I don't know why or how but I knew I had to get to my crystals, it took me so long. I was afraid they'd come back. But I made it to my stash and instantly I knew which crystals would heal my bones, which would heal my cuts and which wold heal my bruises. When the guys returned and saw me shivering on the floor hugging crystals almost fully healed they freaked. They called my step-father and he ran upstairs, already furious that they had probably killed me. When he realised that I was gifted with new age healing he held off the beatings and said if I hired out my skills to his friends then he would let that be the end of my nonsense, I had no choice but to agree, I knew if he let Danny and the others near me again they would keep the crystals away and I would die! The day you came I was so scared cause my step-brothers were planning on going out to find chicks and were waiting for Danny to fly in from home, I was so afraid and then you came. You saved me! From the cleansing plague, from my family, from Danny, from killing myself. You save me Tobias and I will never forget it." She finally looked at him and saw he was sobbing now, so hurt for her. He still didn't speak, just kissed her forehead and snuggling into her more, moving her slightly so they could spoon more comfortably.

Tobi didn't know how long he clung to Luca, both of them sobbing and holding each other tight as Tobi was rocked by Luca's confession. She was raped, by a man she trusted, by her step brothers, she watched her mother be raped by her step father, she had been beaten near to death and no one had helped her. He was glad he had ripped the men apart; he wished he had spent longer taking them apart, bit by bit, so their suffering was immense. He held back growling and snarling, not wanting to scare her when she was this venerable. She slowly started to shake less, relaxing back into him and he breathed a sigh of relief that she trusted him, it was awe inspiring and so humbling that after all she had been through she still trusted him, a huge, probably terrifying creature with a high sex drive and yet she clung to him, trusted him, loved and mated him. Tobi hugged her slightly harder, trying not to cry again. Luca wriggled in his arms and he felt a bolt of terror that he had hugged her too tightly but she just turned in his arms to wrap around him with her arms and legs.

"Please Tobi, either say something or kiss me, I am terrified I have freaked you out. Now you know everything about me and it's not pleasant. I've seen and done horrible things, been used in horrific ways and yet you haven't ran from me. I attacked you in my sleep and you still hold me close. So please, Tobias, I love you, I am your mate, right now, I need mind blowing sex to clear my mind of this horrible nightmare or I need you to talk to me, to tell me it's all alright. Please baby, love me." He couldn't think of anything to say without making things awkward so he kissed her, slow and gentle. He showed how he loved her with soft and gentle movements, kisses, slowly bring them together to rock together, both of them crying softly as they stared into each other's eyes as they brought their bodies together and rocked together till they shuddered with ultimate bliss. They wrapped around each other and neither moved for a long time. At the back of Tobi's mind he knew he had training today but he couldn't leave Luca yet, not yet.

Luca remembered vaguely waking up to say goodbye as Tobi sneaked out of the room to go training at seven, she had snuggled down further under the duvet, the chilling winter morning making it hard to want to leave the warm nest she and Tobi had made. Her alarm went off at nine and she hissed at it, realising she was picking up bad habits from Dom and Jadar about hissing when emotional. She struggled her way out of the covers and sluggishly pulled on her leggings and a vest top, grabbing some of Tobi's sweatpants and hoodies she decided that a dance would wake her up and keep her mind clear of last night's nightmare. Before she left the room she moved the dream catcher from the window to the bed and hung more crystals at the window instead. She left, munching on a banana as she strolled to the communal area, knowing where the gym was. Walking into the reception she glanced round nervously but the receptionist smiled welcomingly.

"Hey there. You here for the gym?"

"Erm well yes and no, I'll go to the gym but I was hoping that there was a private room that I could use to dance in, with an iPod dock, if that's possible." Luca walked to the desk and twirled her hair.

"Yeah sure we have one room available on a first come first served basis. Normal the teams use it to train so I know it has lots of mats and the like; it has an iDock as well. You can have it for one hour, two hours, or any half hour between them."

"Erm, can I have it for two hours please, I need a good work out, haven't done anything for ages. Am I allowed to eat and drink in the room, just to check?" The receptionist smiled kindly.

"Of course dear, there's vendors in the corridor just swipe your id card. Also I'll need your name to book the room out." Luca fumbled in her pockets, knowing she had grabbed her horrible id card with the picture of her hung over after the party the first night. "Oh they got you to? Don't worry, i'm grinning like a goof in mine. All right, I have what I need and you can go right on down. Third door on the right my dear, have fun. The rooms are sound proof so it'll be fine to have your music as loud as you want." Luca grinned and walked more confidently down the corridor and into the room, dumping the hoodies as the room was quite warm she went and got two bottles of Ribena before returned and shutting the door. Plugging in her music she decided to start on a difficult song to dance to, Black Pearl club remix, to really stretch her out and warm her up, as the music started she kicked off the sweats and stretched before throwing herself into the music.

"What do you mean we can't train?" Dominic growled at the female on the reception. "It is our time, let us use our room!" He snarled at her, wanting her immediate submission but she just snarled back, not backing down.

"As I already said two teams can train at once and then the spare room is given out on a first come first served basis. Teams Blue and Sig are training already and a female came in half hour ago and took the spare room for two hours. You will have to wait or use the communal gym."

"Why does one female get a whole training room to herself?" Tobi snapped from the back of the group. He had not enjoyed the run and just wanted to go join Luca back in bed.

"Because she was here first!" The reception female answered with a low warning growl, her patience wearing thin. "If you want to go ask to share it with her then fine. But do not scare her or force her out." Dominic stomped towards the training room, the rest of the team trailing him as Damian had yet to turn up. The sound of pounding bassy dance music blasted out of the door as Dominic snapped it open and froze; the team crowding round to peer past him in to the room. Luca danced, spun and tumbled across the room unaware of her audience. Her hair bounced and a light layer of sweat covered her body as she pushed herself harder, leapt higher and somersaulted further. As one song entered the last seconds of bass she back flipped three times and landed in a perfect side split. The song finished and the next started so she spun to get up. Her foot slipped out from under her on a piece of paper she hadn't noticed and she threw her hands up with a cry as the floor rushed up to meet her face. But it didn't. Strong warm hands grabbed her around the waist and she was scooped up into muscled arms. Tobi glared down at her, taking her breathe away with his ruggedly handsome features, even if at that moment they were disapproving. Unable to control her body she shivered with excitement and looped her arms around his neck, latching onto his mouth and hungrily kissing him, demanding he kiss her back just as hard. The team wolf whistled, making Tobi growl at them and put Luca down to give themself a bit of space.

"Be more careful little firefly, I can't bare you hurting yourself."

"Sorry, I didn't see it. Thanks." She mumbled before looked at his face and arm, the red marks from her scratches that morning still marred his arms and she reached for her crystal to offer to heal him.

"No my firefly, I have to still heal a little on my own, else I'll turn soft." He joked as the team moved into the room.

"Hey Luca, can we have the room now?" Dominic asked as he stomped to the iDock and shut it off, the air ringing with the silence.

"Erm, I have it for another hour don't I? I really need to get this out of my system. If you guys have a full gymnasium I can practice on the bars but if not no, you can't sorry." Luca shuffled uncomfortably at denying the male but she still really needed to centre herself more, her mind still flashing back to the nightmare.

"We do. Jadar can take you there, he ran the slowest." Damian ordered as he walked in the room, his face hard. "We need to train harder than normal and we need this room, sorry Luca. But if you're happy with the bars in the gym upstairs then it'll all be good. Don't argue Tobi, shit just got real!" Tobi shut his mouth and grumbled softly before hugging Luca and pushing her gently towards the door. Grabbing her outer clothes, iPod and drinks she trailed Jadar from the room, feeling self-conscious as the males watched them go.

"What was that about?" Tobi growled when the door had shut behind her.

"Just got out of a meeting with Woden and the other team leaders, we have serious shit going down. A new General has taken over the Border States and he's a mean fucker. This is all we know so listen up. He was one of the first mutants created in the lab, not changed by the plague. He's high up enough to have his own minions, who aren't linked to the professors hive mind. It seems he's been placed in the Border States as the professor has heard that we saved a female free Hu and he feels that there might be more in the area. I pray there are not for their sakes, it seems they are being used as experiments to see why they are not carriers and if they can bear carrier children and if their children will be immune to. The professor takes great delight in testing on females as well we know and the General is apparently very good at it. His name, we think, is General Cheng." Damian snarled and glared at each member of his team. "He cannot find where we are, he cannot harm any free Hu, especially a female and he will not find his stay easy. We are to go tomorrow to Washington and see what we can find out. No arguments. I'm sorry Tobi but we have been ordered to do this, and think; if we can scare him off or slow him down then Luca will be safer for a while." Tobi nodded, even though he didn't agree. "Now, enough talk, we have to train hard and get rid of any slackness we have picked up on our break, we cannot afford to be slack!"

Luca glanced around the now quiet living room as it calmed after the males had bundled out a few minutes ago, they were being posted and it terrified her. She had almost begged Damian to let her go as team medic and he had down right refused. Tobi had taken her to one side to explain that there was a General of the professors' causing a storm and that they had to go deal with him but it was a short, covert mission so it should work out to be that they came back within five days, she had yelled at him that she didn't care he was so far away why did they have to bother with him. When Tobi had left he hadn't looked back and Luca had felt like hell. Luca pulled her knees up and hugged them, allowing herself some time to wallow in fear and self-pity of being left alone, it seemed most of the teams had left, making the entire base seem quieter. This morning Luca had felt weak and shaky, and she had assumed it was from nerves that the males were leaving but now she felt overwhelmingly dizzy and was glad she was already sitting down. She curled onto her side and whimpered, wanting Tobi back. A rattling at the door made her think Tobi had returned for her and she bolted upright but the dizziness was over powering and she fell forwards, crashing into the coffee table. Moment's later soft hands where cradling her, checking her over as voices called for a medic and for Tobi and the team to return immediately. She tried to wave them off but at that moment the queasiness that had been mildly present since she had awoken took over and she emptied her stomach onto the floor.

"Always flipping carrots." She muttered before fainting dead away in Starbrights arms. The next time she was fully conscious she was wrapped in a blanket in Tobi's arms on the sofa, a cold flannel on her forehead and a hovering crowd of worried males. Starbright was next to her, kneeling on the floor and she shushed everyone as Luca looked at her confused. "Hey, what happened? The guys had left." Luca's voice came out in a dry croak and she coughed horrible. Starbright offered her a straw and Luca gladly sucked up some ice cold water. Feeling better she shifted to look at Tobi. "Really, what's up?"

"You don't remember *Winyan wanagi*. You yelled at me this morning and then we left. Starbright came to check on you and you had fainted, threw up then fainted again. You have fever my love. You're scaring me." Luca stopped herself from saying it wasn't her fault, unsure why she was feeling so tender and bitchy.

"I remember you leaving, I was upset, I thought Starbright was you returning and I stood up too fast. Then carrots." She trailed off realising she had thrown up on Starbright.

"No worries, I dodged most of it." Starbright answered her unasked question cheerfully, offering her more water. "Now my question is, why faint and hurl in the first place, you have enough crystals on you to jingle like a Christmas tree." She was concerned and couldn't hide it, making Luca worry more.

"I don't know, I have just been feeling dizzy recently, it's nothing major i'm sure, just done too much, change of diet, all of the above." She babbled, trying not to shake as a cold chill took over. Tobi hugged her tighter though as he could feel her shiver.

"Starbright, she needs more warmth." He growled, desperately trying to remain calm even as he panicked about his mate.

"Guys i'm fine, a little dizzy, it's nothing major please stop fussing me it's annoying. You guys are supposed to be on a mission. Shoo and I'll go sleep it off ok." Luca huffed, trying to get out of Tobi's hold, as this was going on Patch walked in uncomfortably.

"Hay Luca, erm... I need to talk to you privately and I know you've been ill so Tom and Toby want to come over and I really need to talk to you now!" He shifted nervously as all the creatures in the room turned to glare at him.

"Why are you here free Hu, my mate is ill and does not need you near her. How have you heard about her anyway when she has not seen you." At that Luca shifted uncomfortably.

"Erm, Tobi, me and Patch have been chilling quite a lot recently, I've been teaching him how to dance better and stuff." Tobi couldn't hold back his growl.

"You have been meeting a man and not told me of this?"

"Well no, first it wasn't any concern of you, two, it was just Patch so chill and three your amazing sense of smell didn't already tell you of our meetings?" She answered sarcastically, feeling mean but needing to lash out. Tobi shifted her off him and stalked away to the kitchen and Luca rose unsteadily to her feet. "Let's talk in the garden." She and Patch left the living room and everyone behind them. Luca stomped to a bench and settled on it, still feeling dizzy again at the brief time of being upright. Patch sat next to her and looked at her concerned.

"Luca, why are you picking fights with Tobi, you love him so much."

"I don't know Patch; I just need to snap at him, I feel so stressed and grumpy. I keep feeling dizzy and sick and want to curl up and die and everyone is hovering over me like i'm going to pop my clogs any moment and it scares me cause i have no idea why!" Patch shushed her and hugged her to his side, stroking her hair.

"Hey, chill lover its fine. Every girl has this stage a month."

"But it's not the monthly, i'm behind, and that scares me. But i'm being silly and you're news is more important, how did it go?"

"I haven't asked yet, i'm too afraid, I have it in my pocket but it's awkward, we've been bickering and i'm worried as Toby would then be left out and... I just don't know." It was Luca's turn to hug Patch and they sat for a moment, both thinking about how the problems in their lives had changed so much. The sliding door opened again and a nervous Tom looked out.

"Oh hey there, erm..." he walked over to them biting his thumb. "It's tense in there, what's up Luca?" He asked, kneeling in front of them and hugging them both.

"I feel ill, Patch needs to man up and you smell nice." Luca summed up briefly, worried at Tobi stalked out of the living room glaring daggers at the two men hugging her. "Oh shut it before you even start you over bearing male. They are my friends and on a stronger note, they are both gay you pig headed idiot so way not interested in me." She stood up and pushed Patch towards Tom. "Man up and do it, stop being afraid of it, life is too damn short and it obviously takes a lot to make people realised you are committed to them as calling them mate is not enough obviously." She ranted at Tobi, fed up of his mistrust, she was his mate, and there was nothing else she could do to commit to him more in his culture. Tobi looked hurt and Tom was downright confused. Patch shuffled then dropped to his knees in front of Tom.

"Well this is nowhere near how I wanted it but Luca is right, I have to man up and do it instead of planning the shit out of it and missing out. Tom, I know we have only been together for a few short weeks and that our situation is confusing at most but I know in my deepest parts of my heart that you are they guy for me, you're sweet and funny and I want to commit to you on the deepest level of relationship the doomed Human race has left. I want you to agree to marry me Tom, please, say yes." He drew from his inner pocket a small velvet box and popped it open, a loop of silver with a streak of gold running through the middle of it, a discrete ruby so dark it looked like an onyx gem embedded in the centre. Tom was speechless and Luca felt herself start crying as Tobi encircled her in his arms. Luca wanted to be mad at him but the moment was too special and she hugged him back hard, tugging him away from the now embracing couple. The team looked confused as they walked back in, trying to peer past them to see into the garden but Tobi gestured for them not to, letting the men have their privacy. Everyone was still worried over Luca but Starbright shushed them, worried they'd make her more annoyed.

"Damien, it seems to have been a false alarm, Luca looks much better so it was just a dizzy spell, you guys need to go before you miss the boat. I'll look after her, really. Tobi, leave her be her nerves are frayed with all you fussing over her with no explanation. And telling her half theories will only make it worse so back off. Go. She'll be fine with me and the guys." Luca looked sharply at her.

"Ok yes I feel better and yes they should go but please don't keep me in the dark like I don't deserve to be respected enough to understand things like a child. I know I keep snapping and sulking but please, tell me." The team shuffled and looked to Tobi who looked at his feet and at her slowly, worrying etched across his face.

"Luca, my W*inyan wanagi*, we are worried because you shouldn't be ill, the only reason you'd have to be ill is if the plague is affecting you. We have never met a free Hu woman so we have no idea how you react to the plague, we know the men can't get infected but women, maybe we never find any because they get infected by a secondary effect of the plague before we can save them and then they are taken when they are weak. We don't know. We can't tell what is wrong with you as your scent hasn't changed. It worries me so much, leaving you alone right now, even with Starbright and the guys. I'm sorry I judged them but I am possessive and dominating and I was worried I hadn't noticed that you were spending time with them. I'd be even more worried that I can't scent anything at all if the guys hadn't scented anything either." He looked so scared that Luca had to hug him, even if at the moment he was driving her insane she needed to reassure him.

"Tobi I shower after dancing, me and Patch say goodbye before we head off to the changing rooms so there's no reason his scent would stay with me is there?"

"Well no..." Tobi looked to the side, mumbling sulkily that he hadn't realised this.

"So relax, if I smell healthy then I am healthy. I'll nap today, the guys and Starbright and I can have a sleepover party and I won't spend any time alone I swear. Then when you get back we can deal with your over dominating nature when it comes to my gay best friends! Well, Toby is straight but he doesn't, he's still, something happen when he was in Iraq and he's not, he isn't interested is what i'm trying to get to." It took some time but the guys were persuaded to leave again and Starbright set about organizing stuff for a BBQ afternoon. Luca went up to hers and Tobias' room and curled on the bed, letting his familiar scent wash over her. Luca felt one hundred per cent better but what they had said about the plague and their lack of understanding still scared her. She hugged his pillow tight to her stomach and breathed deep, trying to remain practical. She felt fine; it was just a dizzy spell. Laying there she starred up at her dream catcher, letting her mind wander till with a bang her brain lit up like a light bulb. Her crystals could tell her if she as ill! She face palmed herself and darted to the chest of drawers, her box of spare crystals sat next to a picture of Luca and Tobi on the picnic they went on a few weeks ago. The photo shower changed to the team posing beside the pool and Luca grinned, she loved these guys and she wanted to be able tell them when they returned exactly what was wrong or right with her. She'd even go with Starbright to the medical centre and let them run tests so everything could be cleared. Tobi and the team hadn't considered she could just have had food poisoning or a cold so it was probably that. Scoping up some crystals she held them close to her stomach, the place most upset this morning and sat patiently as they heated and she felt their different elements flare and explore her body. Nothing happened for quite some time and then, one by one, the crystals all started projecting a happy blue light sensation to Luca, then changing to a pink light sensation, back and forth over and over and when Luca pushed for more information as to what was wrong they just glowed happier and brighter and started humming annoying childhood chants. Getting infuriated at them she put them back in the chest and ignored them. Starbright called up that she could use some help with the salad and that Toby had arrived so Luca shrugged off the strange lingering sense of contentment and went down stairs to discuss her plans of going to the medical centre tomorrow.

An unpleasant surprise

The next morning Luca woke up squeezed between the sofa, Starbright and Toby. Last night she had taken one sofa, the happily engaged couple the other and Toby on the floor with Starbright. Somehow Luca had rolled off the sofa and Toby had rolled onto of her and Starbright. He was a lump. Groaning and poking his ribs Luca got him to roll away finally and she only just made it to the kitchen sink in time to hurl again. Instantly Toby was awake and shoving Starbright and they both rushed to her side, rubbing her back and worrying over her head.

"Oi gay couple! Get up and call medical, we're heading in fast. Luca is not well!" Toby yelled in military mode, his hand jabbing at them then the phone in a comically militaristic way. Starbright ran upstairs to grab Luca some clothes and she hurriedly dressed in the downstairs bathroom with Starbright standing in the door in case she fainted. Toby had the jeep running as Starbright carried her out under protest and Tom and patch said they'd tidy the house then meet them at the medical centre in a few so as not to crowd the doctors. Toby would have broken nearly every driving law Canada had if there was still a law system in place and skidded to a halt outside the medical centre where a doctor and two creature male nurses waited for them. Starbright refused to let her go and Luca was kinda glad, her head was reeling and she thought she might throw up again at any moment. Starbright carried her to a private examination room and Toby was forced to wait outside to his disapproval.

"Now Luca, tell me exactly how you feel right now?" The doctor asked as he and the nurses scrubbed their hands and sorted out the machines on the wall. One of the nurses hooked her up to a blood pressure and heart rate monitor as the other helped her strip into a hospital gown.

"Dizzy, and like, I need to throw up. My head's light and my tummy's churning but that could be cause of the sterile smell in here. Is it really necessary to do all this, i'm ok." The doctor nodded and pushed her back onto the bed gently.

"Luca, we're all very worried for you, feeling like this for two days in a row is not good or normal and we need to understand why. We're going to take blood and urine samples and then keep you in for observation. We might run a cat scan if the samples don't give us much to go on. We are going to take a bit of blood so we can run quick general tests but also so we can do tests that take longer. Just relax; once we've taken everything we need you to eat and drink plenty and your friends can stay with you." Luca sighed and lay back on the bed again, trying to stay calm as the nurses took three vials of blood and then made her go to the toilet in a Tupperware container. They left her alone after that, letting Toby, patch and Tom in with Starbright and the gathered round her in the bed.

"So, sleepover part two, in the hospital!" Joked Patch, making everyone relax a bit more, they all had worried expressions and kept glancing at each other.

"So, wedding to plan and all that." Luca said loudly. "Can I be the maid of honour and Toby be the best man? Whose who anyway?" She winked at Tom making him blush.

"We're both wearing jeans so no ideas about dresses! It's just casual, simple, and effective." He replied making everyone laugh. They kept gossiping about wedding plans, having to explain most of the finer points to Starbright whose knowledge of weddings was limited to say the least. It was a few hours later, when they were wading into the murky depths of food for the guests, when the doc walked back in, looking if anything more worried.

"Luca, can I speak to you alone please." Everyone filed out slowly, throwing looks over their shoulders as they went to get a coffee whilst the doc spoke to her. "Luca, I know you are mated to a creature so I know he has a highly active sex drive. Tell me, what species is he?" Luca looked confused at him.

"He's canine. Not sure what species though." The doctor looked even more worried Luca feared he'd faint.

"So his sense of smell is significantly better than the rest of the group you are in, yes?" Luca nodded. "Has he ever mentioned you going into heat or had a high sex drive?" Luca blushed, that was what was said on the boat when Tobi and Dom had fought over her. "I'll take that as a yes. Did he not think to explain what would probably happen, or do you use protection?" Shaking her head she wondered where the doc was going with this, did she have an STD or something? "Ok, so, Luca. When a woman goes into heat her chances of conceiving greatly increase. Most of the creatures cannot conceive for one reason or another, we're working on a cure but it seems sperm rate for them is not as high as it needs to be. However, in your case it seems that it was plenty high enough or you had intercourse a significant amount of times to allow you to conceive. Basically Luca, what I am trying to tell you is that you're pregnant, the first pregnancy for creatures ever, and I have no idea what is happening. Tell me, when did you go into heat?" Luca's head reeled and she struggled to think to answer the question.

"Erm, well, I think it was, erm, about two months ago, just before I got here I think. But I haven't felt anything or suspected or. How? I mean, I didn't even notice I missed my period!" Luca blushed and flustered.

"Well, all I can say is you seem to be progressing at a faster pace than expected, it seems your baby is displaying attributes to the father, canine pregnancy is a lot shorter than human pregnancies, you're almost half way through. I want to run more tests, please, come with me." The doc carefully removed all the wires Luca was hooked to and helped her stand. He kept an arm around her waist as they walked towards the back of the centre. Luca started to worry, well worry over something not related to the crazy fact she was pregnant, when they walked into a sort of loading bay at the very rear of the medical centre. She slowed but the doctor kept pulling her forward towards a man standing next to a car. The man opened the boot and Luca felt pure fear lurch through her body. The doc sneered down at her, his hold going from caring to painful, pinching her skin to pick her up and restrain her as the other man guided her kicking body in the boot of the car. She gathered breathe to let lose a scream but the doc cuffed her round her head, making her feel weak and stunning her, giving them time to shove her in the boot. Her arms were wedged against her body and the bags filling the boot. The doc withdrew a syringe and jabbed her hard with it, her head instantly filling with a cloudy haze. The men blurred and she went limp, never having let loose a scream. The next few days passed in a drugged haze for Luca, she didn't know how they got her off the base, but they did. They had driven for most of the day then stopped to camp out in the wood. Luca was let out of the boot to go to the toilet and then was given a snack bar. She gulped the water they gave her and then didn't even struggle when they loosely tied her hands and feet to either door in the back of the car and then the doc stabbed her with the needle again, sending Luca back into the world of unconsciousness.

Tobi was petrified, they had gone to America and returned in a matter of days, it had been a waste as there was no sign of General Cheng and only a few crazed carriers hanging around. Tobi had walked back into their house and searched for Luca but no one was in, going downstairs again he growled as Starbright and the guys were talking in low voices.

"Where is my mate?" He snarled, smelling their fear and worry.

"Tobias. Calm. She has been taken. Woden has been trying to track those that took her. The car they used was found dumped at the border. The car scented of drugs, sedatives, but that was all. One of the docs at the medical centre seems to have been a free Hu working for the professor; apparently he pays well for information on us." Tobi wanted to howl and run to track down the people who took his mate, his Luca, but instead his legs gave out. Damian grabbed him as his knees buckled and he fell to the floor.

"I need her Dam, I need her now." Tobi was ashamed he was shaking but couldn't stop, his fear taking over.

"Tobi, listen carefully, we are tracking them, we will find them, we will save her. Bu you must be prepared. First, you know the professor, you know the General's reputation, and you know she isn't going to have it easy. But there's worse news. Tobias, are you listening? The medics checked the tests he had run on her when she went to the medical centre; they found why she is so important to them. She pregnant Tobi, pregnant." Tobi's head reeled and he was unable to comprehend Damian's word fully. Luca couldn't be pregnant; he would have scented it on her. But then she had smelt funny before he left. A whining noise came from his throat and he let it, knowing his team wouldn't judge him for showing fear; they too appeared petrified for their friend's mate. Tobi knew he needed to get a grip, get up and get moving but first he ran to his and Luca's room and dived head first into the little nest she had made. He inhaled and finally let loose the howl that had been filling him up since he had heard the words, 'she's gone'. He took up her scent and clung to it, hunting around for her purple triangle scarf. He twisted into and tied it around his neck. Prepared he went back downstairs,

"Let us be going, we have to get back into America, now."

Luca awoke confused; her limbs spread and tied down. Her head felt like it had been kicked by a horse, then tramped by a herd of stampeding cattle. Her mouth was bone dry and her arm was dreadfully sore. She struggled to open her eyes so stopped trying, letting her head calm and her other senses work out what was happening. Her nose burnt with a sharp sterile smell, her back was naked against a metal table but a coarse blanket covered her front. Her arms and legs were held by metal loops. She could hear the hum of machines and the soft rumble of voices from a nearby room. None of it sounded recognisable to her but then, there was also a roaring of the sea in her ears and that was not a literal sound; that was because of her head wanting to break open. A door opened near her and two voices moved closer.

"She's been unconscious for a long time now, do you not need to wake her up, there are multiple questions I have for her and I am not a patient man." The first voice stopped next to her and Luca felt his gaze on her, holding back a shudder with great trouble. The other man, for Luca could tell they couldn't be women for some reason, spoke from her other side.

"I have told you sir, it is impossible to force her to wake as there is no reason for her to sleep. We can wait and run all the lab tests we want, when she wakes you may talk to her but till then she is in my domain." It seemed the first man had more authority generally but the second man was in charge of the lab. Luca didn't want to talk to the first man, but the second wanted to experiment on her unconscious body. The heavier footed man walked away and the man on her left leant over her.

"I know you are awake woman. Open your eyes or I shall take this blanket off you and enjoy examining your luscious body as painfully for you as possible." Luca flinch as he lifted the blanket off her thigh. She struggled to open her eyes again, they were gunky and heavily lidded but he stopped uncovering her. Her eyes watered at the harsh light about her head and she blinked rapidly, her breathe hitching as the man's face swam into view. He had tightly scrapped back black hair; his olive skin seemed paled under the fluorescent tubes. His face was pitted with scars and his eyes were black, starring at her with a hard, expressionless expression.

"Wakey wakey woman. You have been a naughty girl haven't you? Running away with a dog, spreading your legs to breed with it and now carrying its bastard litter. You need to be taught a lesson, but at the same time you are invaluable to us, we need more creatures to use, and if you are compatible enough to have pups then perhaps you are compatible with our drugs to make you a creature yourself. Now that would be interesting, how would that affect the things growing inside you? You are defiantly a feline at heart, so, I think a cute domestic cat would suit you, mix it in with your natural submissive nature. Oh yes, I know all about that from a mutual friend, although he doesn't yet know you are here, it will be, interesting, I am sure." His voice was like oil, sticking on her skin and making her feel dirty. She hated it, and him, instantly. But she knew her best chance of survival was to watch and wait, nothing they did would be rapid, she hoped. She was confused as to whom he referred to as their mutual friend, scared he had one of her friends locked up somewhere. "Listen carefully Luca, yes I know your name, I know everything about you. I want you to behave whilst the Doctor examines you and then you and I shall have a talk about that horribly primitive base you have been living on for the past two months. I look forward to hearing about how the beast mounted you." He laughed, more like an evil villain than Luca cared to imagine as he left the room, the large Doctor returning. He looked like the doc at the medical centre and as Luca thought of him he appeared behind the chubby man, leering down at her. Without warning the Doctor whipped the blanket off her body, exposing her pale flesh to their perverted gaze as they took their time perusing her naked flesh. They started at her feet, examining every part of her, taking scrap samples every now and then, their touch lingering as they moved up her body. They reached her crotch and she screamed at them, trying to get away from their rough touch, going everywhere, taking swab samples and letting their hands rest against her private area for a long time, talking to each other and licking their lips, their eyes darting from her to the door. Luca screamed again and the doc pinched her inner thigh, making her cry out and her eyes water.

"Shut it bitch, we're not allowed to do anything to you. You're too important, as are the things inside you. So quiet and we'll behave, mostly. If not we can make this a lot more uncomfortable for you." Luca fell quiet, scared of what they would do. They moved up her body finally and Luca tensed. They spent even more time on her breasts and Luca felt tears slip down her face, but she didn't make a sound, she wouldn't make this any more pleasurable for them than it already was. They pulled out some of her hair and then left her, bare and sobbing softly. The first man walked back and Luca finally placed his origin, he was a Hawaiian islander, and he was staring at her again.

"So, you do not like the doctors, I understand, lab technicians when I met them, now they are responsible for so much, the Professor was a fool to trust them but things progress. Now little Luca, come with me." He undid the cruel metal restraints and threw a set of scrub like clothes at her. She pulled them on and tried to wipe her face at the same time, not wanting to look weak. He led her from the sterile room and down a white corridor, passing labs and examination rooms. They reached a lift and it took them up to a sort of command centre, it looked out across a metal town, linked by metal walkways and bridges, they looked like cargo containers butchered to become living quarters and store houses. Luca was amazed at the number of people walking around, all with blank faces and no care for each other, they didn't bump into each other but there was no chatter, no recognition, acknowledgment that there was anyone else on the same walkway. It scared Luca slightly, the deadness in their eyes. The people in the command centre were similar but they acknowledged each other as they had to work together, discussing supplies, cities that were infected, apocalyptic or deserted. It seemed by the boards they were working on that all of the United States of America was over thrown, most of Mexico and it was spreading further south. It was strange to see Europe and the rest of the world was fine, but Iceland was completely covered, making Luca think that was where the plague has started. The islander was waiting beside a terminal, waiting for her to join her patiently, he looked like he enjoyed watching her face fall, as she realised the extent of the plague. She walked to him, not wanting to displease him, she didn't know who he was but he was a man with power and it was never a good idea to annoy one of those, hopefully he would give her information about the place they were and what he planned to do with her in more detail, letting Luca know if she would ever have a chance to escape. He gestured for her to step in front of him and she saw there was a shadowy man on the terminal in front of him. He, like the islander, made her instantly afraid, and she could hardly see more than his face. It was hard and pale, like he had never been outside in his life, his eyes were almost clear, like ice and his hair was slicked back silver, he was like an ice demon whereas the man behind Luca was a demon of the sun. The man on the screen seemed confused to see her and spoke in a harsh voice like a chain smoker.

"Who is this Cheng, she is not one of the free Hu's you have presented me before, and you found a new one? Brilliant!"

"It is better than that Professor; she is a pregnant free Hu."

"Ah you intend to experiment on the genes of her and her baby to see why they are immune yes?"

"Yes and no Professor. She is a free Hu, pregnant by a creature. Her child is a half breed." The Professor starred at her open mouthed before smiling like a Cheshire Cat.

"Oh really, well that is significantly interesting. So much so I believe I shall come see her in person."

Cheng's reflection in the terminal screen as it shut

off was almost comical if Luca wasn't so terrified. Not only was the Professor personally coming to meet her but the man behind her was the dreaded General Cheng, like the others she had been stupid to believe like his name he would be oriental but instead he was a full blooded islander, and he was more intimidating than Lucas's worst fears. He took her arms and pulled her away.

"So you are interesting enough to make the Professor leave the safety of the citadel, intriguing. I will have to speed up the experiments to make sure he is pleased with all our progress. Come, now." He swept from the room and back to the lift, down to the lab area again. He shoved her through a door and made her lay back on a table. "Time to start your change Luca, time to embrace your inner creature. I wonder if it will change the species of your child, it would be highly interesting to our research; a child that young should be highly susceptible to our drugs, making the breeding of more creatures very easy. We do need a new army, and the creatures will be unable to attack their new brethren." The general was smiling broadly, a completely unnatural expression for his expressionless face so it looked like he was in agony. He let her as the Doctor walked in with a tray full of syringes and vials, making Luca struggle, her inane fear of needles making her keen in panic. The Doctor laughed and put a strap over her forehead, pinning her completely and preventing her from seeing anything else. The vials clinked and Luca felt him swipe a swap across her inner arm and then the sharp pinch of a needle going in to her skin, just below her elbow. Luca couldn't tell how many things he injected into her but her body started to burn and itch after the first minute, she moaned with the pain and the Doctor lent over to look at her face.

"That was just the first drug, I have ten more, and then the change drugs, and then some neo natal drugs to make sure your precious baby is at the peak of its health." It took almost an hour for him to feed all of the vials of drugs into her; she thought she had passed out at some points. The last vial felt like her burning blood was frozen and she definitely passed out this time. The next time she opened her eyes she was on a small military bed like the kind her real father had when she still saw him. She fought off tears at that unbidden memory, she never thought of her father, he was long gone and never looked back. Movement behind her made her whip round, something in retrospect she wished she hadn't done, and she fell off the bed and retched. Soft hands fluttering on her, stoking her back and trying to help her upright.

"It's ok it's ok I felt the same after the first lot of drugs, it wears off and if it doesn't, well then you'll die like the others, so please man up and let it wear off." A feminine sing-song voice jarred though Luca's fussy brain. She worked with her to get back on the bed and fell back into the flat pillow. A vision of blonde stereotypical beauty leaned over her with a worried expression. "Hey there, you're the first woman in a while, they keep dying and I'm not changing so I get kept alive to be experimented on more. So sorry but you need to live cause one more freaking session with Doc perv and his needles and I'll kill myself! It's someone else's turn!" The women stood up and went back to her cot, leaving Luca to wallow in self-pity and pain. She wished she had her crystals, they would help her.

Tobi growled and paced below the ridge, waiting for Damian and Dom to return from scouting out an effective route through the temporary town they had tracked the kidnappers and Luca to. Tobi was angry and restless, it had taken too much time already, they had had her for almost eighteen days, ten of them inside the town of plagued humans with general Cheng. The team was joined by three others, the operation being high importance that a plague town had sprung up so close to the old Canadian border worried Woden. The safe zone was less safe than it should be. All of the team were uptight and impatient to go in and save Luca, but then team in charge had more level heads, a full plan was needed before they would risk the lives of creatures. Tobi spun as he heard Damian return.

"Are we going? Is the route clear? What Damian!"

"Calm, yes we are going in now, the plagued are all unconscious in their sleep state so we can sneak past. The building in the centre is where we believe Luca is, we couldn't see any guards but I'm, sure there are plenty. Listen Tobi, she might be in a bad shape when we get there and I need you to keep a lid on your vengeful rage, she'll need you calm and cuddly so no manic bathing in anyone's blood, no matter what has happened. Understand?" Tobi grunted, impatient to go now they had the go ahead. Starbright and her team appeared next to him.

"Let's go, Tobi, my girls are going to get Luca, so you can follow us, Woden thinks it might be better if she sees a female first and then you, just in case she's too traumatised to recognise you as anything but a huge male." Tobi growled and nodded, willing to agree to anything to make them stop talking and move. They started moving into the plague town, all bare footed to prevent any clinking or excess noise of hard impacts on the metal walkways. It was simple to move from container to container, putting a silenced round in any plague human they found on the way. It was hard, no matter their aim, killing apparently sleeping women and children made it hard on all of them, there were many soft curses and threats to the Professor for causing this irradiation of the human kind. It took almost an hour for the four teams to clear the town and meet up at the entrance to the main building. Operation leader gestured and they burst through the doors, pinging above their head made them dive for cover as the three plague humans shot at them. One creature wasn't fast enough and took a round to the leg, going down in the open. Dom and Tobi had gone for the same cover and were closest to him so as Tobi returned fire round the corner they hid behind Dom slid out on his stomach and dragged the moaning creature into cover with them. Letting the other teams deal with the plague humans Tobi and Dom quickly poured congealment powder onto the wound, bandaged it tight and stabbed a needle full of antibiotics and painkillers into the male's arm. The wound was a through and through hole on the edge of his thigh, it didn't seem to have damaged any arteries so he should live. Leaving him propped against the wall, the medic checking their work, they moved down the corridor after the rest of the team. They and Starbright's team went down a flight of stairs as the other two went up a flight. Damian was waiting for them in a harshly lit white corridor, organising pairs to search each branch of the floor. Tobi and Dom moved down the left branch, Starbright and another female behind them.

They swept three rooms before finding anyone. Two men in lab coats were cowering behind a counter in a lab. Not wanting to waste any time Tobi and Dom plastic cuffed them to the table and left them there, the creatures were snuffling and sneezing as they finished their search as the men had wet themselves with fear. Nothing on their corridor, making Tobi snarl loudly. Checking in with the others, they too had only found a few lab technicians but no Luca. The teams above were engaging in a heavy fire fight so Damian took all but Tobi, Dom, Starbright and her female battle buddy up to help them. Tobi stalked back to the doctors, knowing they would have the information he needed. He was shocked to find the younger, thinner one gone. Grabbing the fat one by the throat he growled and the man screamed, answering before Tobi even had to ask.

"The door at the back, both women are in there. He wanted to kill them before you could get them. He's crazy! I just do this for a job but he loves it!" Tobi threw him to the floor and heard something crack, probably his skull against the edge of the counter but he didn't care, he was already moving to the door to rip it open and howl in horror at the sight of his very pregnant mate huddled unmoving in a corner as another female attacked the second doctor, she had blood in her platinum hair but it wasn't hers, as Dom and Starbright joined him the doctor went down as the female ripped his throat out with her teeth. She growled and scampered in front of Luca to protect her, baring her teeth at the creatures, assuming they were another threat. Starbright pushed the two males back and crouched, making soft calming noises at the female to calm her.

"It's alright; we're here to help, here to save you from this place. I'm Starbright and Luca is my very good friend, please, can you tell me that she's ok?" Starbright wanted the female to realise Luca needed help badly enough to trust them. Instead the female growled louder.

"Of course she's not ok, she's near going into labour, her DNA has been screwed around with and I think that included the babies. We're both screwed, last week we were both human women, now we're half breed mutants like you!" She wasn't rude deliberately, just angry and scared. Looking at her more carefully they noticed her slightly orange eyes and extended canines. She was feline it seemed, but half done, her fangs were small and her muscled less formed then on Starbright. Tobi kept trying to star past her petrified as Luca still hadn't moved or made a sound.

"Luca! My W*inyan wanagi,* I'm begging you, please, move, tell me you're alive. Mate of my soul I need you please!" His voice broke, he didn't want to attack the newly created female but his Luca was more important. She glared at him.

"Are you Tobias?"

"Yes, please, let me be near my mate, I beg. I beg!" He fell to his knees, submitting to a dent in his pride as he pleaded to be able to get to his mate.

"You can come closer, just you though." She moved to the left and Tobi was instantly past her and cradling Luca. Her stomach was huge from the pregnancy and her pulse fluttered. Tobi growled to see her features had been mutated as well, feline, and a lot larger a change than the blonde female. Lucas's parted lips revealed sharp little teeth and canines like a cat and her hair had a streak of turtle black colour through it like a domestic cat. Her breathing was erratic and as he lifted her to cuddle her to his chest she moaned softly in pain, her eyes fluttering open but not focusing. She moaned again and her head fell backwards as she black out again.

"Get the medic down here now!" He growled, trying to make her comfortable to stop her pain. She tensed in his arms and like a possessed woman her eyes opened and rolled back as she shrieked, her body going into labour as her water broke. "Now!" Tobi yelled at Dom standing still with shock at the door. He ran off and Tobi lifted Luca into his arms as he stood making her scream in pain again. "Sorry my love sorry you need to be on a bed I'm sorry." He kept saying it over and over, ignoring the female and Starbright as he strode back past the still body of the doctor and to the room next door where there was a metal bed and medical equipment. As gently as he could he laid her onto the bed and ripped off her sodden scrub bottoms. He stroked her head and stomach, trying to help as her body tensed over and over, getting more rapid as the contractions came closer together. Luca screamed and cried and Tobi knew he was sobbing as well, praying and begging for her to see, for help, cursing himself for making her pregnant, for not protecting her enough. Starbright was there to, trying to see if the baby was coming out or not. The medic ran in and blanched, hurrying to grab a pair of gloves and moving to her exposed lower half. The rest of the team ran in after him with Dom leading them. The medic yelled at them to get Tobi out of the room as the secondary medic joined them. Starbright was allowed to stay. Tobi fought to stay but they bundled him out and locked the door. Luca had fallen silent and this scared Starbright more than the screaming. The medic had his hands inside her, moving the baby's head and he was talking to Luca, telling her what to do, when to push. No one knew how long the medics and Starbright were in the room, it seemed like hours to Tobi but eventually a soft crying sound drifted into the corridor followed by louder screams of a healthy and unhappy baby. The medic undid the door and let a very frazzled Tobi into the room to see Luca laying still on the table and behind her Starbright holding two bundles, his children, wrapped in ripped up blanket. The other medic was clearing up and the first patted Tobi's arm.

"It's ok mate, it's ok. We had to sedate her, she was too hysterical. The twins are fine, male and female and boy, they're fully creatures alright. Canine and feline, the female DNA seems more susceptible to alteration apparently. Luca doesn't look that healthy though, I need to get them home but it should all be fine, you have to trust me and the doctors back at base to fix her." Tobi looked through him slightly, unable to fathom what was going on past he had children, creature children. He was so excited but at the same time afraid, they could be the death of Luca. He went to her first, stroking her hair and nuzzling her. Her scent had changed, become more creature than free Hu and she also smelt of disinfectant and blood. He picked her up gently and turned to Starbright.

"Take care of them, till Luca can. And if she dies, I don't want them." Everyone gasped at him but he didn't care, he walked out of the room and took Luca home.

New beginnings.

Luca awoke from a horrible nightmare she thought. She had been kidnapped and experimented on till she was more domestic kitten than human. She had been pregnant and they had only been three months old when they demanded to come out of her. There had been a woman, a blonde beauty who had bullied Luca to keep fighting. They had both been changed. She remembered hearing Tobi yelling for her and then the doc coming in and punching her, she had hit her head as she fell to the floor hard and had gone into labour. She thought Tobi had begged someone to let him near her and then it all went red and black in a haze of agony. Luca started and opened her eyes, reaching for Tobi and finding him at her side like always. He looked so tired and worried even in his sleep that she had to kiss him, she tried to roll over to be on top of him to make him smile but something tugged against her hand, stopping her. She gasped and saw an IV drip in her hand. Taking in the room they were in she realised they weren't home in bed but in a room of the medical centre. Luca was so confused and needed Tobi's reassurance, shaking him violently. He started awake and growled before realising it was her shaking him. He enveloped her in a tight hug and Luca felt so many bruises covering her body, and then wetness on her neck and thighs. Her neck, she discovered was wet because Tobi was crying, clinging to her like he was holding her onto this life. She hugged him back, trying to smooth him even as her stomach cramped and she moaned. He instantly let go, climbing off her bed and rushing to the door to yell for a doctor. Luca tried to move the blankets off her but Tobi distracted her, holding her hands and stroking her face, looking so immensely relieved that Luca got scared.

"Tobi, what's going on? What's been happening? Why am I in medical? Last I remember I was here cause I was throwing up. Is it the plague? Am I infected? What is it?!" Tobi wouldn't look at her and that made everything worse. A doctor and some nurses rushed it and shooed Tobi out. They fused over Luca; she had been bleeding which was why her thighs had become wet. Luca saw her stomach and was confused at the stretch marks and added weight. Her head hurt so much, things that seemed like reality were a dream and her dreams seemed like reality. The doctor gave her more painkillers and she blurred out, the last thing she heard was the nurse talking about panic attacks being dangerous for her weaken heart.

Next time Luca awoke she knew everything. Her brain had calmed and she remembered all of it. The sessions with the Doctor getting drugged and altered, the 'talks' with the general where he tried to torture information about the base out of her. But more importantly Luca knew she had given birth to twins and she wanted them right now. The nurse sitting next to her was shocked when she jerked up right and screamed at him that she wanted her mate and babies. He fled from her instantly, leaving Luca to spend the minutes he was gone trying to analyse what had changed about her. Her mouth felt funny, almost too full and when she felt around her teeth they all seemed sharper. Her canines felt like what Tobi's looked like, elongated. Her vision was better as was her hearing so she heard the whispered argument the nurse and doctor were having at the end of the corridor.

"She's awake and she remembers and she wants her babies"

"Brilliant but she needs rest and Tobias doesn't want the children so how are we going to get them to her and give her rest without him flipping out again. From what I hear he's been a terror to everyone, he put Dominic and Jadar in here yesterday because they yelled at him for ignoring his kids. How is he going to react when he hears she wants them? I think it best to calm her down, give her mild sedatives to make her relax then let her and Tobias talk is out."

"There are still too many drugs in her system, giving her anything more might be a dreadful idea."

"But letting her have the babies and then making Tobias come see her will result in an argument I doubt she can handle right now." The doctor moved closer to the nurse Luca thought. "Please, trust me, we need to let her see and talk to Tobias before anything else happens." The nurse signed but backed down, moving down the corridor, Luca guessed he was going to get Tobi. She felt so many different emotions, but most of them negative towards Tobi. Why would he not want their children? Was something wrong with them? Did he not want anything to do with either them or Luca since they had been experimented on? Who knew what the drugs had done to their little bodies. Luca held back a sob, she didn't want Tobi. She just wanted her children. Her breasts felt heavy and instinct told her that the babies would be hungry, would need breast feeding. She tore the IV out of her arm and got unsteadily to her feet. She was in a new hospital gown and when she had stopped seeing the world through a kaleidoscope of sights, sounds and smells that overwhelmed her as she stood Luca stepped out of the doors and into the corridor. She saw Damian's back to her further down the corridor, away from the aggravating doctor. Walking towards him she found herself stalking, cat like instead of walking like she used to. Luca thrilled in the power she felt coursing through her muscles. Damian didn't turn round and Luca stood right behind him.

"They are just so cute, how can he hate them Starbright?"

"He doesn't really hate them. What he said was I should care for them until Luca could, but if she died then he wouldn't want them. To me, that means that if he doesn't have Luca to support him he couldn't bear to see her in the children every day. No one else in a team has a mate; those that are mated are possessive and obsessed with each other. But none of them have had children so we don't know how they feel about the children. If they love them like their mates, if they have space to love anyone else. For all we know Tobi meant he didn't want to be heartbroken, he could know that without his mate he might never be able to fully be alive again and he might, in a recess of his mind, know that the children would be better off with me then a father that is dead inside, that cannot look at them as they look too much like his lost love." Damian and Starbright were looked through a window into the nursery.

"But that isn't the case is it? I'm alive and well. So where is he and why haven't I been allowed to see my babies yet? I could get quite angry and I am dying to try out my new muscles." Luca felt a purr in her throat and blushed, embarrassed that they seemed to be uncontrollable. She laughed though as Starbright and Damian seemed to jump a meter in the air and spin in the air at the same time. She could hear their hearts and Luca couldn't stop before she moved closer to Starbright, sniffing and tilting her head side to side as her eyes picked up different colours and her ears heard picked up little rustles of clothing. Starbright held still and Luca looked at her confused. "What? Is this how you feel all the time? So many sights and sounds and smells. It's amazing!" Starbright let her breath out in a huff.

"Wow Luca you scared us. You're really quiet. Erm, the docs wanted to keep you alone till they did a mental competency test. And well, they worried about how you'd react to seeing small children with your instincts in over drive the way they are at the moment with all the new sights and sounds." Luca was surprised she was so calm, able to smile and shrug instead of getting angry.

"Instincts? Just the overload of sights and sounds. And anyway, pretty sure I was mixed with a domestic cat, and they all love children." Starbright looked uncomfortable and Damian grinned at her.

"Wow Luca, you're defiantly not domestic, but then again, nurturing mothers are very scary. You can come see them through here and we'll take it from there." Luca stepped forward between the siblings and stared through the glass at the two cots facing them. On the left was a sleeping male, sucking his thumb and his lashes fluttering against his cheek as he dreamed. His soft auburn hair looked like tightly coiled springs and his nose was flatten slightly, looking very canine. Luca's daughter was in the cot on the right. She was sitting up and blowing bubbles, giggling to herself. Her eyes were a glittering green and her hair was so long for a baby, such a wonderful deep black hair made her naturally tanned skin showed her joint American Indian background from both parents. The male's skin was only slightly darker than white. Luca purred again and pawed the glass, wanting to touch them, hold them.

"You haven't named them yet, have you?" Luca said with a hitch in her voice. Starbright hugged her to her side.

"Of course not sweetie. That's for you and Tobias, they're yours and we don't want to take them from you ever."

"Please, let me hold them." Luca turned to plead with Damian and saw Tobi behind him at the end of the corridor. "Oh." Damian and Starbright turned with her and all three stood protectively in front of the window as Tobi growled towards them. He stopped just in front of Luca and stared at her hard. Starbright and Damian slowly walked away and left them to it, Starbright reassuring Damian that it would be safe. Luca didn't say anything and nor did Tobi. They stood watching each other till Luca sighed and opened her arms. Immediately Tobi tackled her and snuggled against her, shoving his face against her neck and breathing in her scent hard. She did the same, wrapping around him and breathing him in deeply. They clung to each other and then Tobi turned them so they could both watch the antics of their children through the glass. The male had woken up and had thrown a rattle at his sister who in turn was now trying to jump out of her cot to attack him.

"Seems they take after their creatures a lot, already walking, already scrapping, they're gonna be hell, always. Just think how bad it's going to be when they hit the toddler tantrum years, or the teenage years!" Tobi shook in mock terror, making Luca laugh. The babies stopped their antics and looked at the window, hearing their laughter. "They recognise us do you think?" His voice had taken on an air of awe. Luca smiled and touched the glass, gasping as both babies lifted their hands to mimic them. "Ok screw what the doctors say about mental evaluations and shit. Wanna go hold our kids?" Tobi said carrying Luca towards the door. Inside they were met by soft puppy growls and purrs as their children sat up and waited for them. Tobi wouldn't let Luca down but past her both babies before settling himself on the floor. Their daughter instantly started to climb all over them, having fun exploring whilst their son curled up on Luca's lap and growled happily as she hugged him to her. The doctor, Damian, Starbright, Dominic, Jadar, Tom, Patch and Toby found them that way when they came in to see what the loud purring sound was. All four of them were purring and snuggled together, Luca and Tobi laughing as the kids either play fought each other or Tobi. They had ganged up on him and Luca was laughing hard as Tobi got baby feet in his mouth and kidneys.

"You named them yet?" Starbright asked Luca, grinning at her.

"Crystal and Duluth, after beautiful, powerful objects in nature and the place we met." There were groans and cries of baby abuse but everyone just kept grinning at the happy family. They all bundled Luca, Tobi and the babies out of the medical centre before anyone could object too loudly. As they were leaving Patch took Luca's arm.

"Bad timing but me and Tom are thinking of getting married this weekend, what you think?" Luca smiled, starling him at her sharp feline teeth.

"Oh I think we can plan something by then." She laughed, full of confidence and life, the past behind her, the future bright and exciting.

18621037R00127

Made in the USA
Charleston, SC
13 April 2013